FACE TO FACE WITH DEATH

The Rebel officer raised his electrobinoculars and focused on the objects resolutely advancing through the snow, looking like creatures out of the past . . . But they were war machines, each of them stalking like enormous ungulates on four jointed legs—the Empire's All Terrain Armored Transports!

The officer grabbed his comlink. "Rogue Leader—Incoming! Point Zero Three!"

"Echo Station Five-Seven, we're on our way." Even as Luke Skywalker replied, an explosion sprayed ice and snow around the officer and his terrified men.

D0980976

STAR WARS: THE EMPIRE STRIKES BACK™

Starring

| Mark Hamill | Harrison Ford | Carrie Fisher |

Billy Dee Williams   Anthony Daniels
as C-3PO

Co-starring

David Prowse
as Darth Vader

Kenny Baker
as R2-D2

Peter Mayhew
as Chewbacca

Frank Oz
as Yoda

Directed by
Irvin Kershner

Produced by
Gary Kurtz

Screenplay by
Leigh Brackett and Lawrence Kasdan

Story by
George Lucas

Executive Producer
George Lucas

Music by
John Williams

Production Designer
Norman Reynolds

Conceptual Artist
Ralph McQuarrie

Director of Photography
Peter Suschitzky

Film Editor
Paul Hirsch

Special Visual Effects
Brian Johnson and Richard Edlund

Filmed in Panavision® —Color by Rank Film Laboratories
A Lucasfilm Ltd. Production—A Twentieth Century-Fox Release

Recorded in Dolby Stereo

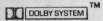 DOLBY SYSTEM ™

by Donald F. Glut

Based on a story by George Lucas

A Del Rey Book

BALLANTINE BOOKS • NEW YORK

A Del Rey Book
Published by Ballantine Books

Library of Congress Catalog Card Number: 80-80518

ISBN 0-345-28392-9

Manufactured in the United States of America

First Edition: May 1980

Cover art by Roger Kastel, supplied by Lucasfilm Ltd.

I

"NOW this is what I call cold!" Luke Sky-walker's voice broke the silence he had observed since leaving the newly established Rebel base hours earlier. He was astride a Tauntaun, the only other living being as far as the eye could see. He felt tired and alone, and the sound of his own voice startled him.

Luke as well as his fellow members of the Rebel Alliance took turns exploring the white wastelands of Hoth, gathering information about their new home. They all returned to base with mixed feelings of comfort and loneliness. There was nothing to contradict their earliest findings that no intelligent lifeforms existed on this cold planet. All that Luke had seen on his solitary expeditions were barren white plains and ranges of blue-tinged mountains that seemed to vanish in the mists of the distant horizons.

Luke smiled behind the masklike gray bandana that protected him against Hoth's frigid winds. Peering out at the icy wastes through his goggles, he pulled his fur-lined cap down more snugly about his head.

One corner of his mouth curled upward as he tried to visualize the official researchers in the service of the Imperial government. "The galaxy is peppered with settlements of colonizers who care little about the affairs of the Empire or its opposition, the Rebel Alliance," he thought. "But a settler would have to be crazy to stake his claims on Hoth. This planet doesn't have a thing to offer anyone—except *us*."

The Rebel Alliance had established an outpost on the ice world little more than a month before. Luke was well-known on the base and, although barely twenty-three years old, he was addressed as *Commander* Skywalker by other Rebel warriors. The title made him feel a bit uncomfortable. Nonetheless, he was already in the position of giving orders to a band of seasoned soldiers. So much had happened to Luke and he had changed a great deal. Luke, himself, found it hard to believe that only three years ago he was a wide-eyed farm boy on his home world of Tatooine.

The youthful commander spurred his Tauntaun. "Come on, girl," he urged.

The snow-lizard's gray body was insulated from the cold by a covering of thick fur. It galloped on muscular hind legs, its tridactyl feet terminating in large hooked claws that dug up great plumes of snow. The Tauntaun's llamalike head thrust forward and its serpentine tail coiled out behind as the beast ran up the ice slope. The animal's horned head turned from side to side buffeting the winds that assaulted its shaggy muzzle.

Luke wished his mission were finished. His body felt nearly frozen in spite of his heavily padded Rebel-issue clothing. But he knew that it was his choice to be there; he had volunteered to ride across the ice fields looking for other lifeforms. He shivered as he looked at the long shadow he and the beast cast on the snow. "The winds are picking up," he thought. "And these chilling winds bring unendurable temperatures to the plains after nightfall." He was tempted to return to the base a little early, but he knew the importance of establishing the certainty that the Rebels were alone on Hoth.

The Tauntaun quickly turned to the right, almost throwing Luke off-balance. He was still getting used to riding the unpredictable creatures. "No offense," he said to his mount, "but I'd feel a lot more at ease in the cockpit of my old reliable landspeeder." But for this mission, a Tauntaun—despite its disadvantages—was the most efficient and practical form of transportation available on Hoth.

When the beast reached the top of another ice slope, Luke brought the animal to halt. He pulled off his dark-lensed goggles and squinted for a few moments, just long enough for his eyes to adjust to the blinding glare of the snow.

Suddenly his attention was diverted by the appearance of an object streaking across the sky, leaving behind a lingering trail of smoke as it dipped toward the misty horizon. Luke flashed his gloved hand to his utility belt and clutched his pair of electrobinoculars. Apprehensive, he felt a chill that competed with the coldness of the Hoth atmosphere. What he had seen could have been man-made, perhaps even something launched by the Empire. The young commander, still focused on the object, followed its fiery course and watched intently as it crashed on the white ground and was consumed in its own explosive brilliance.

At the sound of the explosion, Luke's Tauntaun shuddered. A fearful growl escaped its muzzle and it began to claw nervously at the snow. Luke patted the animal's head, trying to reassure the beast. He found it difficult to hear himself over the blustering wind. "Easy, girl, it's just another meteorite!" he shouted. The animal calmed and Luke brought the communicator to his mouth. "Echo Three to Echo Seven. Han ol' buddy, do you read me?"

Static crackled from the receiver. Then a familiar voice cut through the interference. "Is that you, kid? What's up?"

The voice sounded a little older and somewhat sharper than Luke's. For a moment Luke fondly recalled first meeting the Corellian space smuggler in that dark, alien-packed cantina at a spaceport on Tatooine. And now he was one of Luke's only friends who was not an official member of the Rebel Alliance.

"I've finished my circle and I haven't picked up any life readings," Luke spoke into his comlink, pressing his mouth close to the transmitter.

"There isn't enough life on this ice cube to fill a space cruiser," Han answered, fighting to make his voice heard above the whistling winds. "My sentry markers are placed. I'm heading back to base."

"See you shortly," Luke replied. He still had his eye on the twisting column of dark smoke rising from a black spot in the distance. "A meteorite just hit the ground near here and I want to check it out. I won't be long."

Clicking off his comlink, Luke turned his attention to his Tauntaun. The reptilian creature was pacing, shifting its weight from one foot to the other. It gave out a deep-throated roar that seemed to signal fear.

"Whoa, girl!" he said, patting the Tauntaun's

head. "What's the matter . . . you smell something? There's nothing out there."

But Luke, too, was beginning to feel uneasy, for the first time since he had set out from the hidden Rebel base. If he knew anything about these snow-lizards, it was that their senses were keen. Without question the animal was trying to tell Luke that something, some danger, was near.

Not wasting a moment, Luke removed a small object from his utility belt and adjusted its minia-ture controls. The device was sensitive enough to zero in on even the most minute life readings by detecting body temperature and internal life sys-tems. But as Luke began to scan the readings, he realized there was no need—or time—to continue.

A shadow crossed over him, towering above by a good meter and a half. Luke spun around and suddenly it seemed as if the terrain itself had come to life. A great white-furred bulk, perfectly camou-flaged against the sprawling mounds of snow, rushed savagely at him.

"Son of a jumpin' . . ."

Luke's hand blaster never cleared its holster. The huge claw of the Wampa Ice Creature struck him hard and flat against his face, knocking him off the Tauntaun and into the freezing snow.

Unconsciousness came swiftly to Luke, so swiftly that he never even heard the pitiful screams of the Tauntaun nor the abrupt silence following the sound of a snapping neck. And he never felt his own ankle savagely gripped by his giant, hairy at-tacker, or felt his body dragged like a lifeless doll across the snow-covered plain.

Black smoke was still rising from the depression in the hillside where the air-borne thing had fallen.

The smoky clouds had thinned considerably since the object had crashed to the ground and formed a smoldering crater, the dark fumes being dispersed over the plains by the icy Hoth winds.

Something stirred within the crater.

First there was only a sound, a droning mechanical sound swelling in intensity as if to compete with the howling wind. Then the thing moved— something that glinted in the bright afternoon light as it slowly began to rise from the crater.

The object appeared to be some form of alien organic life, its head a multiorbed, skull-like horror, its dark-lensed blister eyes training their cold gaze across the even colder reaches of wilderness. But as the thing rose higher from the crater, its form showed it clearly to be a machine of some sort, possessing a large cylindrical "body" connected to a circular head, and equipped with cameras, sensors, and metal appendages, some of which terminated in crablike grasping pincers.

The machine hovered over the smoking crater and extended its appendages in various directions. Then a signal was set off within its internal mechanical systems, and the machine began to float across the icy plain.

The dark probe droid soon vanished over the distant horizon.

Another rider, bundled in winter clothing and mounted on a spotted gray Tauntaun, raced across the slopes of Hoth toward the Rebel base of operations.

The man's eyes, like points of cold metal, glanced without interest at the domes of dull gray, the myriad gun turrets and the colossal power generators that were the only indications of civilized life on this world. Han Solo gradually slowed his snow-lizard, guiding the reins so the creature trotted through the entrance of the enormous ice cave.

Han welcomed the relative warmth of the vast complex of caverns, warmed by Rebel heating units that obtained their power from the huge generators outside. This subterranean base was both a natural ice cave and a maze of angular tunnels blasted from a solid mountain of ice by Rebel lasers. The Corellian had been in more desolate hell-holes in the galaxy, but for the moment he couldn't remember the exact location of any one of them.

He dismounted his Tauntaun, then glanced around to watch the activity taking place inside the mammoth cave. Wherever he looked he saw things being carried, assembled, or repaired. Rebels in gray uniforms rushed to unload supplies and adjust equipment. And there were robots, mostly R2 units and power droids, that seemed to be everywhere, rolling or walking through the ice corridors, efficiently performing their innumerable tasks.

Han was beginning to wonder if he were mellowing with age. At first he had had no personal interest in or loyalty to this whole Rebel affair. His ultimate involvement in the conflict between Empire and Rebel Alliance began as a mere business transaction, selling his services and the use of his ship, the *Millennium Falcon*. The job had seemed simple enough: Just pilot Ben Kenobi, plus young Luke and two droids, to the Alderaan system. How could Han have known at the time that he would also be called on to rescue a princess from the Empire's most feared battle station, the Death Star?

Princess Leia Organa . . .

The more Solo thought about her, the more he realized how much trouble he eventually bought himself by accepting Ben Kenobi's money. All Han had wanted originally was to collect his fee and rocket off to pay back some bad debts that hung over his head like a meteor ready to fall. Never had he intended to become a hero.

And yet, something had kept him around to join Luke and his crazy Rebel friends as they launched the now-legendary space attack on the Death Star. Something. For the present, Han couldn't decide just what that something was.

Now, long after the Death Star's destruction, Han was still with the Rebel Alliance, lending his assistance to establish this base on Hoth, probably the bleakest of all planets in the galaxy. But all that was about to change, he told himself. As far as he was concerned, Han Solo and the Rebels were about to blast off on divergent courses.

He walked rapidly through the underground hangar deck where several Rebel fighter ships were docked and being serviced by men in gray assisted by droids of various designs. Of greatest concern to Han was the saucer-shaped freighter ship resting on its newly installed landing pods. This, the largest ship in the hangar, had garnered a few new dents in its metal hull since Han first hooked up with Skywalker and Kenobi. Yet the *Millennium Falcon* was famous not for its outward appearance but for its speed: This freighter was still the fastest ship ever to make the Kessel Run or to outrun an Imperial TIE fighter.

Much of the *Falcon*'s success could be attributed to its maintenance, now entrusted to the shaggy hands of a two-meter-tall mountain of brown hair, whose face was at the moment hidden behind a welder's mask.

Chewbacca, Han Solo's giant Wookiee copilot, was repairing the *Millennium Falcon*'s central lifter when he noticed Solo approaching. The Wookiee stopped his work and raised his face shield, exposing his furry countenance. A growl that few non-Wookiees in the universe could translate roared from his toothy mouth.

Han Solo was one of those few. *"Cold* isn't the word for it, Chewie," the Corellian replied. "I'll take a good fight any day over all this hiding and freezing!" He noticed the smoky wisps rising from the newly welded section of metal. "How are you coming with those lifters?"

Chewbacca replied with a typical Wookiee grumble.

"All right," Han said, fully agreeing with his friend's desire to return to space, to some other planet—anywhere but Hoth. "I'll go report. Then I'll give you a hand. Soon as those lifters are fixed, we're out of here."

The Wookiee barked, a joyful chuckle, and returned to his work as Han continued through the artificial ice cavern.

The command center was alive with electronic equipment and monitoring devices reaching toward the icy ceiling. As in the hangar, Rebel personnel filled the command center. The room was full of controllers, troopers, maintenance men—along with droids of varying models and sizes, all of whom were diligently involved in converting the chamber into a workable base to replace the one on Yavin.

The man Han Solo had come to see was busily engaged behind a great console, his attention riveted to a computer screen flashing brilliantly colored readouts. Rieekan, wearing the uniform of a Rebel general, straightened his tall frame to face Solo as he approached.

"General, there isn't a hint of life in the area," Han reported. "But all the perimeter markings are set, so you'll know if anyone comes calling."

As usual, General Rieekan did not smile at Solo's flippancy. But he admired the young man's taking a kind of unofficial membership in the Rebellion. So impressed was Rieekan by Solo's qualities that he often considered giving him an honorary officer's commission.

"Has Commander Skywalker reported in yet?" the general inquired.

"He's checking out a meteorite that hit near him," Han answered. "He'll be in soon.'"

Rieekan quickly glanced at a newly installed radar screen and studied the flashing images. "With all the meteor activity in this system, it's going to be difficult to spot approaching ships."

"General, I . . ." Han hesitated. "I think it's time for me to move on."

Han's attention was drawn from General Rieekan to a steadily approaching figure. Her walk was both graceful and determined, and somehow the young woman's feminine features seemed incongruous with her white combat uniform. Even at this distance, Han could tell Princess Leia was upset.

"You're good in a fight," the general remarked to Han, adding, "I hate to lose you."

"Thank you, General. But there's a price on my head. If I don't pay off Jabba the Hut, I'm a walking dead man."

"A death mark is not an easy thing to live

with—" the officer began as Han turned to Princess Leia. Solo was not a sentimental sort, but he was aware that he was very emotional now. "I guess this is it, Your Highness." He paused, not knowing what response to expect from the princess.

"That's right," Leia replied coldly. Her sudden aloofness was quickly evolving into genuine anger.

Han shook his head. Long ago he had told himself that females—mammalian, reptilian, or some biological class yet to be discovered—were beyond his meager powers of comprehension. Better leave them to mystery, he'd often advised himself.

But for a while, at least, Han had begun to believe that there was at least one female in all the cosmos that he *was* beginning to understand. And yet, he had been wrong before.

"Well," Han said, "don't go all mushy on me. So long, Princess."

Abruptly turning his back to her, Han strode into the quiet corridor that connected with the command center. His destination was the hangar deck, where a giant Wookiee and a smuggler's freighter—two realities he did understand—were waiting for him. He was not about to stop walking.

"Han!" Leia was rushing after him, slightly out of breath.

Coolly, he stopped and turned toward her. "Yes, Your Highness?"

"I thought you had decided to stay."

There seemed to be real concern in Leia's voice, but Han could not be certain.

"That bounty hunter we ran into on Ord Mantell changed my mind."

"Does Luke know?" she asked.

"He'll know when he gets back," Han replied gruffly.

Princess Leia's eyes narrowed, her gaze judging him with a look he knew well. For a moment Han felt like one of the icicles on the surface of the planet.

"Don't give me that look," he said sternly. "Every day more bounty hunters are searching for me. I'm going to pay off Jabba before he sends any more of his remotes, Gank killers, and who knows what else. I've got to get this price off my head while I still *have* a head."

Leia was obviously affected by his words, and Han could see that she was concerned for him as well as, perhaps, feeling something more.

"But we still need you," she said.

"We?" he asked.

"Yes."

"What about *you*?" Han was careful to emphasize the last word, but really wasn't certain why. Maybe it was something he had for some time wanted to say but had lacked the courage— no, he amended, the *stupidity*—to expose his feelings. At the moment there seemed to be little to lose, and he was ready for whatever she might say.

"Me?" she said bluntly. "I don't know what you mean."

Incredulous, Han Solo shook his head. "No, you probably don't."

"And what precisely *am* I supposed to know?" Anger was growing in her voice again, probably because, Han thought, she was finally beginning to understand.

He smiled. "You want me to stay because of the way you feel about me."

Again the princess mellowed. "Well, yes, you've been a great help," she said, pausing before going on, ". . . to us. You're a natural leader—"

But Han refused to let her finish, cutting her off in midsentence. "No, your worship. That's not it."

Suddenly Leia was staring directly into Han's face, with eyes that were, at last, fully understanding. She started to laugh. "You're imagining things."

"Am I? I think you were afraid I was going to leave you without even a . . ." Han's eyes focused on her lips, ". . . kiss."

She began to laugh harder now. "I'd just as soon kiss a Wookiee."

"I can arrange that." He moved closer to her, and she looked radiant even in the cold light of the ice chamber. "Believe me, you could use a good kiss. You've been so busy giving orders, you've forgotten how to be a woman. If you'd have let go for a moment, I could have helped you. But it's too late now, sweetheart. Your big opportunity is flying out of here."

"I think I can survive," she said, obviously irked.

"Good luck!"

"You don't even care if the—"

He knew what she was going to say and didn't let her finish. "Spare me, please!" he interrupted. "Don't tell me about the Rebellion again. It's all you think about. You're as cold as this planet."

"And you think you're the one to apply some heat?"

"Sure, if I were interested. But I don't think it'd be much fun." With that, Han stepped back and looked at her again, appraising her coolly. "We'll meet again," he said. "Maybe by then you'll have warmed up a little." Her expression had changed again. Han had seen killers with kinder eyes.

"You have all the breeding of a Bantha," she snarled, "but not as much class. Enjoy your trip, hot shot!" Princess Leia quickly turned away from Han and hurried down the corridor.

II

THE temperature on the surface of Hoth had dropped. But despite the frigid air, the Imperial Probe Droid continued its leisurely drift above the snow-swept fields and hills, its extended sensors still reaching in all directions for life signs.

The robot's heat sensors suddenly reacted. It had found a heat source in the vicinity, and warmth was a good indication of life. The head swiveled on its axis, the sensitive eyelike blisters noting the direction from which the heat source originated. Automatically the probe robot adjusted its speed and began to move at maximum velocity over the icy fields.

The insectlike machine slowed only when it neared a mound of snow bigger than the probe droid itself. The robot's scanners made note of the mound's size—nearly one-point-eight meters in height and an enormous six meters long. But the mound's size was of only secondary importance. What was truly astounding, if a surveillance machine could ever be astounded, was the amount of heat radiating from beneath the mound. The creature under that snowy hill must surely be well protected against the cold.

A thin blue-white beam of light shot from one of the probe robot's appendages, its intense heat boring into the white mound and scattering gleaming snow flecks in all directions.

The mound began to shiver, then to quake. Whatever existed beneath it was deeply irritated by the robot's probing laser beam. Snow began to fall away from the mound in sizable clumps when, at one end, two eyes showed through the mass of white.

Huge yellow eyes peered like twin points of fire at the mechanical creature that continued to blast away with its painful beams. The eyes burned with primeval hatred for the thing that had interrupted its slumber.

The mound shook again, with a roar that nearly destroyed the probe droid's auditory sensors. It zoomed back several meters, widening the space between it and the creature. The droid had never before encountered a Wampa Ice Creature; its computers advised that the beast be dealt with expeditiously.

The droid made an internal adjustment to regulate the potency of its laser beam. Less than a moment later the beam was at maximum intensity. The machine aimed the laser at the creature, enveloping it in a great flaming and smoking cloud. Seconds later the few remaining particles of the Wampa were swept away by the icy winds.

The smoke disappeared, leaving behind no physical evidence—save for a large depression in the snow—that an Ice Creature had ever been there.

But its existence had been properly recorded in the memory of the probe droid, which was already continuing on its programmed mission.

The roars of another Wampa Ice Creature finally awakened the battered young Rebel commander.

Luke's head was spinning, aching, perhaps exploding for all he could tell. With painstaking effort he brought his vision into focus, discerning that he was in an ice gorge, its jagged walls reflecting the fading twilight.

He suddenly realized he was hanging upside down, arms dangling and fingertips some thirty centimeters from the snowy floor. His ankles were numb. He craned his neck and saw that his feet were frozen in ice hanging from the ceiling and that the ice was forming on his legs like stalactites. He could feel the frozen mask of his own blood caked on his face where the Wampa Ice Creature had viciously slashed him.

Again Luke heard the bestial moans, louder now as they resounded through the deep and narrow passageway of ice. The roars of the monster were deafening. He wondered which would kill him first, the cold or the fangs and claws of the thing that inhabited the gorge.

I've got to free myself, he thought, get free of this ice. His strength had not yet returned fully, but with a determined effort, he pulled himself up and reached for the confining bonds. Still too weak, Luke could not break the ice and fell back into his hanging position, the white floor rushing up at him.

"Relax," he said to himself. "Relax."

The ice walls creaked with the ever-louder bellows of the approaching creature. Its feet crunched on the frigid ground, coming frighteningly nearer. It would not be long before the shaggy white horror would be back and possibly warming the cold young warrior in the darkness of its belly.

Luke's eyes darted about the gorge, finally spotting the pile of gear he had brought with him on his mission, now lying in a useless, crumpled heap on the floor. The equipment was nearly a full, unattainable meter beyond his grasp. And with that gear was a device that entirely captured his attention—a stout handgrip unit with a pair of small switches and a surmounting metal disk. The object had once belonged to his father, a former Jedi Knight who had been betrayed and murdered by the young Darth Vader. But now it was Luke's, given him by Ben Kenobi to be wielded with honor against Imperial tyranny.

In desperation Luke tried twisting his aching body, just enough to reach the discarded light-saber. But the freezing cold coursing through his body slowed him down and weakened him. Luke was beginning to resign himself to his fate as he heard the snarling Wampa Ice Creature approaching. His last feelings of hope were nearly gone when he sensed the presence.

But it was not the presence of the white giant that dominated this gorge.

Rather, it was that soothing spiritual presence which occasionally visited Luke in moments of stress or danger. The presence that had first come to him only after old Ben, once again in his Jedi role of Obi-Wan Kenobi, vanished into a crumple of his own dark robes after being cut down by Darth Vader's lightsaber. The presence that was sometimes like a familiar voice, an almost silent whisper that spoke directly to Luke's mind.

"Luke." The whisper was there again, haunt-ingly. "Think of the lightsaber in your hand."

The words made Luke's already aching head throb. Then he felt a sudden resurgence of strength, a feeling of confidence that urged him to continue fighting despite his apparently hopeless situation. His eyes fixed upon the lightsaber. His hand reached out painfully, the freezing in his limbs already taking its toll. He squeezed his eyes shut in concentration. But the weapon was still beyond his reach. He knew that the lightsaber would require more than just struggling to reach.

"Gotta relax," Luke told himself, "relax . . ."

Luke's mind whirled as he heard the words of his disembodied guardian. "Let the Force flow, Luke."

The Force!

Luke saw the inverted gorillalike image of the Wampa Ice Creature looming, its raised arms ending in enormous gleaming claws. He could see the apish face for the first time now, and shivered at the sight of the beast's ramlike horns, the quivering lower jaw with its protruding fangs.

But then the warrior divorced the creature from his thoughts. He stopped struggling for his weapon, his body relaxed and went limp, allowing his spirit to be receptive to his teacher's suggestion. Already he could feel coursing through him that energy field generated by all living beings, that bound the very universe together.

As Kenobi had taught him, the Force was within Luke to use as he saw fit.

The Wampa Ice Creature spread its black, hooked claws and lumbered toward the hanging youth. Suddenly the lightsaber, as if by magic, sprang to Luke's hand. Instantly, he depressed a colored button on the weapon, releasing a blade-like beam that quickly severed his icy bonds.

As Luke, weapon in hand, dropped to the floor, the monstrous figure towering over him took a cautious step backward. The beast's sulfurous eyes

blinked incredulously at the humming lightshaft,
a sight baffling to its primitive brain.

Though it was difficult to move, Luke jumped
to his feet and waved his lightsaber at the snow-
white mass of muscle and hair, forcing it back a
step, another step. Bringing the weapon down,
Luke cut through the monster's hide with the blade
of light. The Wampa Ice Creature shrieked, its
hideous roar of agony shaking the gorge walls. It
turned and hastily lumbered out of the gorge, its
white bulk blending with the distant terrain.

The sky was already noticeably darker, and with
the encroaching darkness came the colder winds.
The Force was with Luke, but even that mysterious power could not warm him now. Every step
he took as he stumbled out of the gorge was more
difficult than the last. Finally, his vision dimming
as rapidly as the daylight, Luke stumbled down
an embankment of snow and was unconscious before he even reached the bottom.

In the subsurface main hangar dock, Chewie was
getting the *Millennium Falcon* ready for takeoff.
He looked up from his work to see a rather curious pair of figures that had just appeared from
around a nearby corner to mingle with the usual
Rebel activity in the hangar.

Neither of these figures was human, although
one of them had a humanoid shape and gave the
impression of a man in knightly golden armor. His
movements were precise, almost too precise to
be human, as he clanked stiffly through the corridor. His companion required no manlike legs for
locomotion, for he was doing quite well rolling
his shorter, barrellike body along on miniature
wheels.

The shorter of the two droids was beeping and whistling excitedly.

"It is *not* my fault, you malfunctioning tin can," the tall, anthropomorphic droid stated, gesturing with a metallic hand. "I did not ask you to turn on the thermal heater. I merely commented that it was freezing in her chamber. But it's *supposed* to be freezing. How are we going to get all her things dried out? . . . Ah! Here we are."

See-Threepio, the golden droid in human shape, paused to focus his optical sensors on the docked *Millennium Falcon.*

The other robot, Artoo-Detoo, retracted his wheels and frontal leg, and rested his stout metal body on the ground. The smaller droid's sensors were reading the familiar figures of Han Solo and his Wookiee companion as those two continued the work of replacing the freighter's central lifters.

"Master Solo, sir," Threepio called, the only one of the robotic twosome equipped with an imitation human voice. "Might I have a word with you?"

Han was not particularly in a mood to be disturbed, especially by this fastidious droid. "What is it?"

"Mistress Leia has been trying to reach you on the communicator," Threepio informed him. "It must be malfunctioning."

But Han knew that it was not. "I shut it off," he said sharply as he continued to work on his ship. "What does her royal holiness want?"

Threepio's auditory sensors identified the disdain in Han's voice but did not understand it. The robot mimicked a human gesture as he added, "She is looking for Master Luke and assumed he would be here with you. No one seems to know—"

"Luke's not back yet?" Immediately Han became concerned. He could see that the sky beyond the ice cavern entrance had grown considerably darker since he and Chewbacca had begun to repair the *Millennium Falcon*. Han knew just how severely the temperatures dropped on the surface after nightfall and how deadly the winds could be.

In a flash he jumped off the *Falcon*'s lift, not even looking back toward the Wookiee. "Bolt it down, Chewie. Officer of the Deck!" Han yelled, then brought his comlink to his mouth and asked, "Security Control, has Commander Skywalker reported in yet?" A negative reply brought a scowl to Han's face.

The deck sergeant and his aide hurried up to Solo in response to his summons.

"Is Commander Skywalker back yet?" Han asked, tension in his voice.

"I haven't seen him," the deck sergeant replied. "It's possible he came in through the south entrance."

"Check on it!" Solo snapped, though he was not in an official position to give commands. "It's urgent."

As the deck sergeant and his aide turned and rushed down the corridor, Artoo emitted a concerned whistle that rose inquiringly in pitch.

"I don't know, Artoo," Threepio answered, stiffly turning his upper torso and head in Han's direction. "Sir, might I inquire what's going on?"

Anger welled up inside Han as he grunted back at the robot, "Go tell your precious princess that Luke is dead unless he shows up soon."

Artoo began to whistle hysterically at Solo's grim prediction and his now-frightened golden partner exclaimed, "Oh, no!"

The main tunnel was filled with activity when Han Solo rushed in. He saw a pair of Rebel troopers employing all their physical strength to restrain a nervous Tauntaun that was trying to break free.

From the opposite end, the deck officer rushed into the corridor, his eyes darting around the chamber until he had spotted Han. "Sir," he said frantically, "Commander Skywalker hasn't come through the south entrance. He might have forgotten to check in."

"Not likely," Han snapped. "Are the speeders ready?"

"Not yet," the deck officer answered. "Adapting them to the cold is proving difficult. Maybe by morning—"

Han cut him off. There wasn't any time to waste on machines that could and probably would break down. "We'll have to go out on Tauntauns. I'll take sector four."

"The temperature is falling too rapidly."

"You bet it is," Han growled, "and Luke's out in it."

The other officer volunteered, "I'll cover sector twelve. Have control set screen alpha."

But Han knew there was no time for control to get its surveillance cameras operating, not with Luke probably dying somewhere on the desolate plains above. He pushed his way through the assemblage of Rebel troops and took the reins of one of the trained Tauntauns, leaping onto the creature's back.

"The night storms will start before any of you can reach the first marker," the deck officer warned.

"Then I'll see you in hell," grunted Han, tugging

the reins of his mount and maneuvering the animal
out of the cave.

Snow was falling heavily as Han Solo raced his
Tauntaun through the wilderness. Night was near
and the winds were howling fiercely, piercing his
heavy clothes. He knew that he would be as useless as an icicle to Luke unless he found the young
warrior soon.

The Tauntaun was already feeling the effects of
the temperature drop. Not even its layers of insu-
lating fat or the matted gray fur could protect it
from the elements after nightfall. Already the beast
was wheezing, its breathing becoming increasingly
labored.

Han prayed that the snow-lizard wouldn't drop,
at least not until he had located Luke.

He drove his mount harder, forcing it on across
the icy plains.

Another figure was moving across the snow, its
metal body hovering above the frozen ground.

The Imperial Probe Droid paused briefly in mid-
flight, its sensors twitching.

Then, satisfied with its findings, the robot gently
lowered itself, coming to rest on the ground. Like
spider legs, several probes separated from the
metal hull, dislodging some of the snow that had
settled there.

Something began to take shape around the robot, a pulsating glow that gradually covered the
machine as if with a transparent dome. Quickly
this force field solidified, repelling the blowing
snow that brushed over the droid's hull.

After a moment the glow faded, and the blowing snow soon formed a perfect dome of white,

completely concealing the droid and its protective force field.

The Tauntaun was racing at maximum speed, certainly too fast considering the distance it had traveled and the unbearable frigid air. No longer wheezing, it had begun moaning pitifully, and its legs were becoming more and more unsteady. Han felt sorry about the Tauntaun's pain, but at present the creature's life was only secondary to that of his friend Luke.

It was becoming difficult for Han to see through the thickening snowfall. Desperate, he searched for some interruption in the eternal plains, some distant spot that might actually be Luke. But there was nothing to see other than the darkening expanses of snow and ice.

Yet there was a sound.

Han drew the reins in, bringing the Tauntaun to an abrupt halt on the plain. Solo could not be certain, but there seemed to be some sound other than the howling of the winds that whipped past him. He strained to look in the direction of the sound.

Then he spurred his Tauntaun, forcing it to gallop across the snow-swept field.

Luke could have been a corpse, food for the scavengers, by the time the light of dawn returned. But somehow he was still alive, though barely, and struggling to stay that way even with the night storms violently assaulting him. Luke painfully pulled himself upright from the snow, only to be blasted back down by the freezing gale. As he fell he considered the irony of it all—a farm boy from

Tatooine maturing to battle the Death Star, now perishing alone in a frozen alien wasteland.

It took all of Luke's remaining strength to drag himself a half meter before finally collapsing, sinking into the ever-deepening drifts. "I can't . . ." he said, though no one could hear his words.

But someone, though still unseen, had heard.

"You must." The words vibrated in Luke's mind. "Luke, look at me!"

Luke could not ignore that command; the power of those softly spoken words was too great.

With a great effort, Luke lifted his head and saw what he thought was a hallucination. In front of him, apparently unaffected by the cold and still clad only in the shabby robes he had worn in the hot desert of Tatooine, stood Ben Kenobi.

Luke wanted to call out to him, but he was speechless.

The apparition spoke with the same gentle authority Ben had always used with the young man. "You must survive, Luke."

The young commander found the strength to move his lips again. "I'm cold . . . so cold . . ."

"You must go to the Dagobah system," the spectral figure of Ben Kenobi instructed. "You will learn from Yoda, the Jedi Master, the one who taught me."

Luke listened, then reached to touch the ghostly figure. "Ben . . . Ben . . ." he groaned.

The figure remained unmoved by Luke's efforts to reach it. "Luke," it spoke again, "you're our only hope."

Our only hope.

Luke was confused. Yet before he could gather the strength to ask for an explanation, the figure began to fade. And when every trace of the ap-

parition had passed from his sight, Luke thought
he saw the approach of a Tauntaun with a human
rider on its back. The snow-lizard was approaching, its gait unsteady. The rider was still too far
away, too obscured by the storm for identification.

In desperation the young Rebel commander
called out, "Ben?!" before again dropping off into
unconsciousness.

The snow-lizard was barely able to stand on its
saurian hind legs when Han Solo reined it to a
stop and dismounted.

Han looked with horror at the snow-covered,
almost frozen form lying as if dead at his feet.

"Come on, buddy," he appealed to Luke's inert
figure, immediately forgetting his own nearly frozen body, "you aren't dead yet. Give me a signal
here."

Han could detect no sign of life, and noticed that
Luke's face, nearly covered with snow, was savagely torn. He rubbed at the youth's face, being
careful not to touch the drying wounds. "Don't do
this, Luke. It's not your time."

Finally a slight response. A low moan, barely
audible over the winds, was strong enough to send
a warm glow through Han's own shivering body.
He grinned with relief. "I knew you wouldn't leave
me out here all alone! We've got to get you out of
here."

Knowing that Luke's salvation—and his own—
lay in the speed of the Tauntaun, Han moved toward the beast, carrying the young warrior limply
in his arms. But before he could drape the unconscious form over the animal's back, the snow-lizard
gave an agonized roar, then fell into a shaggy gray
heap on the snow. Laying his companion down,

Han rushed to the side of the fallen creature. The Tauntaun made one final sound, not a roar or bellow but only a sickly rasp. Then the beast was silent.

Solo gripped the Tauntaun's hide, his numbed fingers searching for even the slightest indication of life. "Deader than a Triton moon," he said, knowing that Luke did not hear a word. "We haven't got much time."

Resting Luke's motionless form against the belly of the dead snow-lizard, Han proceeded to work. It might be something of a sacrilege, he mused, using a Jedi Knight's favorite weapon like this, but right now Luke's lightsaber was the most efficient and precise tool to cut through the thick skin of a Tauntaun.

At first the weapon felt strange in his hand, but momentarily he was cutting the animal's carcass from hairy head to scaly hind paws. Han winced at the foul odor that rose from the steaming incision. There were few things he could remember that stank like a snow-lizard's innards. Without deliberation he tossed the slippery entrails into the snow.

When the animal's corpse had been entirely eviscerated, Han shoved his friend inside the warm, hair-covered skin. "I know this doesn't smell so good, Luke, but it'll keep you from freezing. I'm sure this Tauntaun wouldn't hesitate if it were the other way around."

From the body of the snow-lizard, another blast of entrail-stench rose out of the disemboweled cavity. "Whew!" Han almost gagged. "It's just as well you're out cold, pal."

There wasn't much time left to do what had to be done. Han's freezing hands went to the supply pack strapped to the Tauntaun's back and rummaged through the Rebel-issue items until he located the shelter container.

Before unpacking it, he spoke into his comlink. "Echo Base, do you copy?"

No response.

"This comlink is useless!"

The sky had darkened ominously and the winds blew violently, making even breathing close to impossible. Han fought to open the shelter container and stiffly began to construct the one piece of Rebel equipment that might protect them both—if only for a short while longer.

"If I don't get this shelter up fast," he grumbled to himself, "Jabba won't need those bounty hunters."

III

ARTOO-DETOO stood just outside the entrance to the secret Rebel ice hangar, dusted with a layer of snow that had settled over his plug-shaped body. His inner timing mechanisms knew he had waited here a long time and his optical sensors told him that the sky was dark.

But the R2 unit was concerned only with his built-in probe-sensors that were still sending signals across the ice fields. His long and earnest sensor-search for the missing Luke Skywalker and Han Solo had not turned up a thing.

The stout droid began beeping nervously when Threepio approached him, plodding stiffly through the snow.

"Artoo," the gold-colored robot inclined the upper half of his form at the hip joints, "there's nothing more you can do. You must come inside." Threepio straightened to his full height again, simulating a human shiver as the night winds howled past his gleaming hull. "Artoo, my joints are freezing up. Will you hurry . . . please? . . ." But before he could finish his own sentence, Threepio was hurrying back toward the hangar entrance.

Hoth's sky was then entirely black with night, and Princess Leia Organa stood inside the Rebel base entrance, maintaining a worried vigil. She shivered in the night wind as she tried to see into the Hoth darkness. Waiting near a deeply concerned Major Derlin, her mind was somewhere out on the ice fields.

The giant Wookiee sat nearby, his maned head lifting quickly from his hairy hands as the two droids Threepio and Artoo reentered the hangar.

Threepio was humanly distraught. "Artoo has not been able to pick up any signals," he reported, fretting, "although he feels his range is probably too limited to cause us to give up hope." Still, very little confidence could be detected in Threepio's artificial voice.

Leia gave the taller droid a nod of acknowledgment, but did not speak. Her thoughts were occupied with the pair of missing heroes. Most disturbing to her was that she found her mind focused on one of the two: a dark-haired Corellian whose words were not always to be taken literally.

As the princess kept watch, Major Derlin turned to acknowledge a Rebel lieutenant reporting in. "All patrols are now in except Solo and Skywalker, sir."

The major looked over at Princess Leia. "Your Highness," he said, his voice weighty with regret, "nothing more can be done tonight. The temperature is dropping fast. The shield doors must be closed. I'm sorry." Derlin waited a moment, then addressed the lieutenant. "Close the doors."

The Rebel officer turned to carry out Derlin's order and immediately the chamber of ice seemed to drop even more in temperature as the mournful Wookiee howled his grief.

"The speeders should be ready in the morning,"

the major said to Leia. "They'll make the search easier."

Not really expecting an affirmative reply, Leia asked, "Is there any chance of their surviving until morning?"

"Slim," Major Derlin answered with grim honesty. "But yes, there's a chance."

In response to the major's words, Artoo began to operate the miniature computers inside his barrel-like metal body, taking only moments to juggle numerous sets of mathematical computations, and climaxing his figurings with a series of triumphant beeps.

"Ma'am," Threepio interpreted, "Artoo says the chances against survival are seven hundred twenty-five to one." Then, tilting toward the shorter robot, the protocol droid grumbled, "Actually, I don't think we needed to know that."

No one responded to Threepio's translation. For several prolonged moments there was a solemn silence, broken only by the echoing clang of metal slamming against metal: the huge doors of the Rebel base were closed for the night. It was as if some heartless deity had officially severed the assembled group from the two men out on the ice plains and had, with a metallic bang, announced their deaths.

Chewbacca let out another suffering howl.

And a silent prayer, often spoken on an erstwhile world called Alderaan, crept into Leia's thoughts.

The sun that was creeping over Hoth's northern horizon was relatively dim, but its light was enough to shed some warmth on the planet's icy surface. The light crawled across the rolling hills of snow, fought to reach the darker recesses of the icy gorges, then finally came to rest on what must have been the only perfect white mound on the entire world.

So perfect was the snow-covered mound that it must have owed its existence to some power other than Nature. Then, as the sky grew steadily brighter, this mound began to hum. Anyone observing the mound now would have been startled as the snow dome seemed to erupt, sending its snowy outer covering skyward in a great burst of white particles. A droning machine began pulling back its retractable sensor arms, and its awesome bulk slowly rose from its frozen white bed.

The probe robot paused briefly in the windy air, then continued on its morning mission across the snow-covered plains.

Something else had invaded the morning air of the ice world—a relatively small, snub-nosed craft, with dark cockpit windows and laser guns mounted on each side. The Rebel snowspeeder was heavily armored and designed for warfare near the planet's surface. But this morning the small craft was on a reconnaissance mission, racing above the expansive white landscape and arcing over the contours of the snowdrifts.

Although the snowspeeder was designed for a two-man crew, Zev was the ship's only occupant. His eyes took in a panoramic scan of the desolate stretches below, and he prayed that he would find the objects of his search before he went snow-blind.

Presently he heard a low beeping signal.

"Echo Base," he shouted jubilantly into his cockpit comlink, "I've got something! Not much, but it could be a sign of life. Sector four-six-one-four by eight-eight-two. I'm closing in."

Frantically working the controls of his ship, Zev reduced its speed slightly and banked the craft over a snowdrift. He welcomed the sudden G-force pressing him against his seat and headed the snow-speeder in the direction of the faint signal.

As the white infinity of Hoth's terrain streaked under him, the Rebel pilot switched his comlink to a new frequency. "Echo Three, this is Rogue Two. Do you copy? Commander Skywalker, this is Rogue Two."

The only reply that came through his comlink receiver was static.

But then he heard a voice, a very distant-sounding voice, fighting its way through the crackling noise. "Nice of you guys to drop by. Hope we didn't get you up too early."

Zev welcomed the characteristic cynicism in Han Solo's voice. He switched his transmitter back to the hidden Rebel base. "Echo Base, this is Rogue Two," he reported, his voice suddenly rising in pitch. "I found them. Repeat . . ."

As he spoke, the pilot pulled in a fine-tune fix on the signals winking on his cockpit monitor screens. Then he further reduced the speed of his craft, bringing it down close enough to the planet's surface so that he could better see a small object standing out against the fleecy plains.

The object, a portable Rebel-issue shelter, sat atop a snowdrift. On the shelter's windward side was a hard-packed layer of white. And resting gingerly against the upper part of the snowdrift was a makeshift radio antenna.

But a more welcome sight than any of this was the familiar human figure standing in front of the snow shelter, frantically waving his arms at the snowspeeder.

As Zev dipped his craft for a landing, he felt overwhelmingly grateful that at least one of the warriors he had been sent out to find was still alive.

Only a thick glass window separated the battered, near-frozen body of Luke Skywalker from four of his watchful friends.

Han Solo, who appreciated the relative warmth of the Rebel medical center, was standing beside Leia, his Wookiee copilot, Artoo-Detoo, and See-Threepio. Han exhaled with relief. He knew that, despite the grim atmosphere of the chamber enclosing him, the young commander was finally out of danger and in the best of mechanical hands.

Clad only in white shorts, Luke hung in a vertical position inside a transparent cylinder with a combination breath mask and microphone covering his nose and mouth. The surgeon droid, Too-Onebee, was attending to the youth with the skill of the finest humanoid doctors. He was aided by his medical assistant droid, FX-7, which looked like nothing more than a metal-capped set of cylinders, wires, and appendages. Gracefully, the surgeon droid worked a switch that brought a gelatinous red fluid pouring down over his human patient. This bacta, Han knew, could work miracles, even with patients in such dire shape as Luke.

As the bubbling slime encapsulated his body, Luke began to thrash about and rave deliriously. "Watch out," he moaned. ". . . snow creatures. Dangerous . . . Yoda . . . go to Yoda . . . only hope."

Han had not the slightest idea what his friend was raving about. Chewbacca, also perplexed by the youth's babbling, expressed himself with an interrogative Wookiee bark.

"He doesn't make sense to me either, Chewie," Han replied.

Threepio commented hopefully, "I do hope he's all there, if you take my meaning. It would be most unfortunate if Master Luke were to develop a short circuit."

"The kid ran into something," Han observed matter-of-factly, "and it wasn't just the cold."

"It's those creatures he keeps talking about," Leia said, looking at the grimly staring Solo. "We've doubled the security, Han," she began, tentatively trying to thank him, "I don't know how—"

"Forget it," he said brusquely. Right now he was concerned only with his friend in the red bacta fluid.

Luke's body sloshed through the brightly colored substance, the bacta's healing properties by now taking effect. For a while it appeared as if Luke were trying to resist the curative flow of the translucent muck. Then, at last, he gave up his mumbling and relaxed, succumbing to the bacta's powers.

Too-Onebee turned away from the human who had been entrusted to his care. He angled his skull-shaped head to gaze at Han and the others through the window. "Commander Skywalker has been in dormo-shock but is responding well to the bacta," the robot announced, his commanding, authoritative voice heard distinctly through the glass. "He is now out of danger."

The surgeon robot's words immediately wiped away the tension that had seized the group on the other side of the window. Leia sighed in relief, and Chewbacca grunted his approval of Too-Onebee's treatment.

Luke had no way of estimating how long he had been delirious. But now he was in full command of his mind and senses. He sat up on his bed in the Rebel medical center. What a relief, he thought, to be breathing real air again, however cold it might be.

A medical droid was removing the protective pad from his healing face. His eyes were uncovered and he was beginning to perceive the face of someone standing by his bed. Gradually the smiling image of Princess Leia came into focus. She gracefully moved toward him and gently brushed his hair out of his eyes.

"The bacta are growing well," she said as she looked at his healing wounds. "The scars should be gone in a day or so. Does it still hurt you?"

Across the room, the door banged open. Artoo beeped a cheerful greeting as he rolled toward Luke, and Threepio clanked noisily toward Luke's bed. "Master Luke, it's good to see you functional again."

"Thanks, Threepio."

Artoo emitted a series of happy beeps and whistles.

"Artoo expresses his relief also," Threepio translated helpfully.

Luke was certainly grateful for the robots' concern. But before he could reply to either of the droids, he met with yet another interruption.

"Hi, kid," Han Solo greeted him boisterously as he and Chewbacca burst into the medical center.

The Wookiee growled a friendly greeting.

"You look strong enough to wrestle a Gundark," Han observed.

Luke felt that strong, and felt grateful to his friend. "Thanks to you."

"That's two you owe me, junior." Han gave the princess a wide, devilish grin. "Well, Your Worship," he said mockingly, "it looks like you arranged to keep me close by for a while longer."

"I had nothing to do with it," Leia said hotly, annoyed at Han's vanity. "General Rieekan thinks it's dangerous for any ships to leave the system until the generators are operational."

"That makes a good story. But *I* think you just can't bear to let me out of your sight."

"I don't know where you get your delusions, laser brains," she retorted.

Chewbacca, amused by this verbal battle between two of the strongest human wills he had ever encountered, let out a roaring Wookiee laugh.

"Laugh it up, fuzz ball," Han said good-naturedly. "You didn't see us alone in the south passage."

Until now, Luke had scarcely listened to this lively exchange. Han and the princess had argued frequently enough in the past. But that reference to the south passage sparked his curiosity, and he looked at Leia for an explanation.

"She expressed her true feeling for me," Han continued, delighting in the rosy flush that appeared on the princess's cheeks. "Come on, Your Highness, you've already forgotten."

"Why, you low-down, stuck-up, half-witted, scruffy-looking nerf-herder . . ." she sputtered in fury.

"Who's scruffy-looking?" he grinned. "I tell ya, sweetheart, I must've hit pretty close to the mark to get you hoppin' like this. Doesn't it look that way to you, Luke?"

"Yeah," he said, staring at the princess incredulously, "it does . . . kind of."

Leia looked over at Luke with a strange mixture of emotions showing on her flushed face. Something vulnerable, almost childlike, was reflected in her eyes for a moment. And then the tough mask fell again.

"Oh, it does, does it?" she said. "Well, I guess you don't understand everything about women, do you?"

Luke agreed silently. He agreed even more when in the next moment Leia leaned over and kissed him firmly on the lips. Then she turned on her heel and marched across the room, slamming the door behind her. Everyone in the room—human, Wookiee, and droid—looked at one another, speechless.

In the distance, a warning alarm blared through the subterranean corridors.

General Rieekan and his head controller were conferring in the Rebel command center when Han Solo and Chewbacca burst into the room. Princess Leia and Threepio, who had been listening to the general and his officer, turned in anticipation at their approach.

A warning signal blared across the chamber from the huge console located behind Rieekan and monitored by Rebel control officers.

"General," the sensor controller called.

Grimly attentive, General Rieekan watched the console screens. Suddenly he saw a flashing signal that had not been there a moment before. "Princess," he said, "I think we have a visitor."

Leia, Han, Chewbacca, and Threepio gathered around the general and watched the beeping monitor screens.

"We've picked up something outside the base in Zone Twelve. It's moving east," said Rieekan.

"Whatever it is, it's metal," the sensor controller observed.

Leia's eyes widened in surprise. "Then it can't be one of those creatures that attacked Luke?"

"Could it be ours?" Han asked. "A speeder?"

The sensor controller shook his head. "No, there's no signal." Then came a sound from another monitor. "Wait, something very weak . . ."

Walking as rapidly as his stiff joints allowed, Threepio approached the console. His auditory sensors tuned in the strange signals. "I must say, sir, I'm fluent in over sixty million forms of communication, but this is something new. Must be in a code or—"

Just then the voice of a Rebel trooper cut in through the console's comlink speaker. "This is Echo Station Three-Eight. Unidentified object is in our scope. It's just over the ridge. We should have visual contact in about—" Without warning the voice filled with fear. "What the—? Oh, no!"

A burst of radio static followed, then the transmission broke off completely.

Han frowned. "Whatever it is," he said, "it isn't friendly. Let's have a look. Come on, Chewie."

Even before Han and Chewbacca were out of the chamber, General Rieekan had dispatched Rogues Ten and Eleven to Station Three-Eight.

The mammoth Imperial Star Destroyer occupied a position of deadly prominence in the Emperor's fleet. The sleekly elongated ship was larger and even more ominous than the five wedge-shaped Imperial Star Destroyers guarding it. Together these six cruisers were the most dreaded and devastating warships in the galaxy, capable of reducing to cosmic scrap anything that strayed too close to their weapons.

Flanking the Star Destroyers were a number of smaller fighter ships and, darting about this great space armada, were the infamous TIE fighters.

Supreme confidence reigned in the heart of every crew member in this Imperial death squadron, especially among the personnel on the monstrous central Star Destroyer. But something also blazed within their souls. Fear—fear of merely the sound of the familiar heavy footsteps as they echoed through the enormous ship. Crew members dreaded these footfalls and shuddered whenever they were heard approaching, bringing their much feared, but much respected leader.

Towering above them in his black cloak and concealing black headgear, Darth Vader, Dark Lord of the Sith, entered the main control deck, and the men around him fell silent. In what seemed to be an endless moment, no sounds except those from the ship's control boards and the loud wheezes coming from the ebony figure's metal breath screen were to be heard.

As Darth Vader watched the endless array of stars, Captain Piett rushed across the wide bridge of the ship, carrying a message for the squat, evil-looking Admiral Ozzel, who was stationed on the bridge. "I think we've found something, Admiral," he announced nervously, looking from Ozzel to the Dark Lord.

"Yes, Captain?" The admiral was a supremely confident man who felt relaxed in the presence of his cloaked superior.

"The report we have is only a fragment, from a probe droid in the Hoth system. But it's the best lead we've had in—"

"We have had thousands of probe droids searching the galaxy," Ozzel broke in angrily. "I want proof, not leads. I don't intend to continue to chase around from one side of—"

Abruptly the figure in black approached the two and interrupted. "You found something?" he asked, his voice somewhat distorted by the breath mask.

Captain Piett respectfully gazed at his master, who loomed above him like a black-robed, omnipotent god. "Yes, sir," Piett said slowly, choosing his words with caution. "We have visuals. The system is supposed to be devoid of human forms . . ."

But Vader was no longer listening to the captain. His masked face turned toward an image beamed on one of the viewscreens—an image of a small squadron of Rebel snowspeeders streaking above the white fields.

"That's it," Darth Vader boomed without further deliberation.

"My lord," Admiral Ozzel protested, "there are so many uncharted settlements. It could be smugglers—"

"That is the one!" the former Jedi Knight insisted, clenching a black-gloved fist. "And Skywalker is with them. Bring in the patrol ships, Admiral, and set your course for the Hoth system." Vader looked toward an officer wearing a green uniform with matching cap. "General Veers," the Dark Lord addressed him, "prepare your men."

As soon as Darth Vader had spoken, his men set about to launch his fearful plan.

The Imperial Probe Droid raised a large antenna from its buglike head and sent out a piercing, high-frequency signal. The robot's scanners had reacted to a lifeform hidden behind a great dune of snow and noted the appearance of a brown Wookiee head and the sound of a deep-throated growl. The blasters that had been built into the probe robot took aim at the furry giant. But before the robot had a chance to fire, a red beam from a hand blaster exploded from behind the Imperial Probe Droid and nicked its darkly finished hull.

As he ducked behind a large snow dune, Han Solo noticed Chewbacca still hidden, and then watched as the robot spun around in midair to face him. So far the ruse was working and now *he* was the target. Han had barely moved out of range as the floating machine fired, blasting chunks of snow from the edge of his dune. He fired again, hitting it square on with the beam of his weapon. Then he heard a high-pitched whine coming from the deadly machine, and in an instant the Imperial Probe Droid burst into a billion or more flaming pieces.

". . . I'm afraid there's not much left," Han said over the comlink as he concluded his report to the underground base.

Princess Leia and General Rieekan were still manning the console where they had maintained constant communication with Han. "What is it?" Leia asked.

"Droid of some kind," he answered. "I didn't hit it that hard. It must have had a self-destruct."

Leia paused as she considered this unwelcome

piece of information. "An Imperial droid," she said, betraying some trepidation.

"If it was," Han warned, "the Empire surely knows we're here."

General Rieekan shook his head slowly. "We'd better start to evacuate the planet."

IV

SIX ominous shapes appeared in the black space of the Hoth system and loomed like vast demons of destruction, ready to unleash the furies of their Imperial weapons. Inside the largest of the six Imperial Star Destroyers, Darth Vader sat alone in a small spherical room. A single shaft of light gleamed on his black helmet as he sat motionless in his raised meditation chamber.

As General Veers approached, the sphere opened slowly, the upper half lifting like a jagged-toothed mechanical jaw. To Veers, the dark figure seated inside the mouthlike cocoon hardly seemed alive, though a powerful aura of sheer evil emanated from him, sending a chilling fear through the officer.

Uncertain of his own courage, Veers took a step forward. He had a message to deliver but felt prepared to wait for hours if necessary rather than disturb Vader's meditation.

But Vader spoke immediately. "What is it, Veers?"

"My lord," the general replied, choosing each word with care, "the fleet has moved out of light-speed. Com-Scan has detected an energy field protecting an area of the sixth planet in the Hoth system. The field is strong enough to deflect any bombardment."

Vader stood, rising to his full two-meter height, his cloak swaying against the floor. "So, the Rebel scum are alerted to our presence." Furious, he clenched his black-gloved hands into fists. "Admiral Ozzel came out of light-speed too close to the system."

"He felt surprise was a wiser—"

"He's as clumsy as he is stupid," Vader cut in, breathing heavily. "A clean bombardment is impossible through their energy field. Prepare your troops for a surface attack."

With military precision, General Veers turned and marched out of the meditation room, leaving behind an enraged Darth Vader. Alone in the chamber, Vader activated a large viewscreen that showed a brightly lit image of his Star Destroyer's vast bridge.

Admiral Ozzel, responding to Vader's summons, stepped forward, his face almost filling the Dark Lord's monitor screen. There was trepidation in Ozzel's voice when he announced, "Lord Vader, the fleet has moved out of light-speed—"

But Vader's reply was addressed to the officer standing slightly behind Ozzel. "Captain Piett."

Knowing better than to delay, Captain Piett stepped forward instantly as the admiral staggered back a step, his hand automatically reaching for his throat.

"Yes, my lord," Piett answered respectfully.

Ozzel began to gag now as his throat, as if in the grip of invisible talons, began to constrict.

"Make ready to land assault troops beyond the energy field," Vader ordered. "Then deploy the fleet so that nothing can get off that planet. You're in command now, Admiral Piett."

Piett was simultaneously pleased and unsettled

by this news. As he turned to carry out the orders, he saw a figure that might someday be himself. Ozzel's face was hideously contorted as he fought for one final breath of air; then he dropped into a dead heap on the floor.

The Empire had entered the system of Hoth.

Rebel troops rushed to their alert stations as the warning alarms wailed through the ice tunnels. Ground crews and droids of all sizes and makes hurried to perform their assigned duties, responding efficiently to the impending Imperial threat.

The armored snowspeeders were fueled as they waited in attack formation to blast out of the main cavern entranceway. Meanwhile, in the hangar, Princess Leia was addressing a small band of Rebel fighter pilots. "The large transport ships will leave as soon as they're loaded. Only two fighter escorts per ship. The energy shield can only be opened for a split second, so you'll have to stay very close to the transports."

Hobbie, a Rebel veteran of many battles, looked at the princess with concern. "Two fighters against a Star Destroyer?"

"The ion cannon will fire several blasts which should destroy any ships in your flight path," Leia explained. "When you clear the energy shield, you will proceed to the rendezvous point. Good luck."

Somewhat reassured, Hobbie and the other pilots raced toward their fighter cockpits.

Meanwhile, Han was working frantically to complete welding a lifter on the *Millennium Falcon*. Finishing quickly, he hopped to the hangar floor and switched on his comlink. "All right, Chewie," he said to the hairy figure seated at the *Falcon*'s controls, "give it a try."

Just then Leia walked past, throwing him an angry look. Han looked at her smugly while the freighter's lifters began to rise off the floor, whereupon the right lifter began to shake erratically, then broke partially loose to swing back down again with an embarrassing crash.

He turned away from Leia, catching only a glimpse of her face as she mockingly raised an eyebrow.

"Hold it, Chewie," Han grunted into his small transmitter.

The *Avenger,* one of the Imperial armada's wedge-like Star Destroyers, hovered like a mechanized death angel in the sea of stars outside the Hoth system. As the colossal ship began to move closer to the ice world, the planet became clearly visible through the windows which stretched 100 meters or more across the huge bridge of the warship.

Captain Needa, commander of the *Avenger's* crew, gazed out a main port, looking at the planet when a controller came up to him. "Sir, Rebel ship coming into our sector."

"Good," Needa replied with a gleam in his eyes. "Our first catch of the day."

"Their first target will be the power generators," General Rieekan told the princess.

"First transport Three Zone approaching shield," one of the Rebel controllers said, tracking a bright image that could only be an Imperial Star Destroyer.

"Prepare to open shield," a radarman ordered.

"Stand by, Ion Control," another controller said.

A giant metal globe on Hoth's icy surface rotated into position and angled its great turret gun upward.

"Fire!" came the order from General Rieekan.

Suddenly two red beams of destructive energy were released into the cold skies. The beams almost immediately overtook the first of the racing Rebel transport craft, and sped on a direct course toward the huge Star Destroyer.

The twin red bolts struck the enormous ship and blasted its conning tower. Explosions set off by the blast began to rock the great flying fortress, spinning it out of control. The Star Destroyer plunged into deep space as the Rebel transport and its two fighter escorts streaked off to safety.

Luke Skywalker, preparing to depart, pulled on his heavy-weather gear and watched the pilots, gunners, and R2 units hurrying to complete their tasks. He started toward the row of snowspeeders that awaited him. On his way, the young commander paused at the tail section of the *Millennium Falcon*, where Han Solo and Chewbacca were working frenetically on the right lifter.

"Chewie," Luke called, "take care of yourself. And watch over this guy, will ya?"

The Wookiee barked a farewell, gave Luke a big hug, then turned back to his work on the lifters.

The two friends, Luke and Han, stood looking at each other, perhaps for the last time.

"I hope you make your peace with Jabba," Luke said at last.

"Give 'em hell, kid," the Corellian responded lightly.

The young commander began to walk away as memories of exploits shared with Han rushed to his mind. He stopped and looked back at the *Falcon*, and saw his friend still staring after him. As they gazed at each other for a brief moment, Chewbacca looked up and knew that each was wishing the other the best, wherever their individual fates might take them.

The public address system broke in on their thoughts. "First transport is clear," a Rebel announcer proclaimed the good news.

At the announcement, a cheer burst from those gathered in the hangar. Luke turned and hurried over to his snowspeeder. When he reached it, Dack, his fresh-faced young gunner, was standing outside the ship waiting for him.

"How are you feeling, sir?" Dack asked enthusiastically.

"Like new, Dack. How about you?"

Dack beamed. "Right now I feel like I could take on the whole Empire myself."

"Yeah," Luke said quietly, "I know what you mean." Though there were only a few years between them, at that moment Luke felt centuries older.

Princess Leia's voice came over the address system: "Attention, speeder pilots . . . on the withdrawal signal assemble at South Slope. Your fighters are being prepared for takeoff. Code One Five will be transmitted when evacuation is complete."

Threepio and Artoo stood amid the rapidly moving personnel as the pilots readied for departure. The golden droid tilted slightly as he turned his sensors on the little R2 robot. The shadows playing over Threepio's face gave the illusion that his faceplate had lengthened into a frown. "Why is it," he asked, "when things seem to get settled, everything falls apart?" Leaning forward, he gently patted the other droid's hull. "Take good care of Master Luke. And take good care of yourself."

Artoo whistled and tooted a good-bye, then turned to roll down the ice corridor. Waving stiffly, Threepio watched as his stout and faithful friend moved away.

To an observer, it may have seemed that Threepio grew misty-eyed, but then it wasn't the first time he had gotten a drop of oil clogged before his optical sensors.

Finally turning, the human-shaped robot moved off in the opposite direction.

V

NO one on Hoth heard the sound. At first, it was simply too distant to carry above the whining winds. Besides, the Rebel troopers, fighting the cold as they prepared for battle, were too busy to really listen.

In the snow trenches, Rebel officers screamed out their orders to make themselves heard above the gale-force winds. Troopers hurried to carry out their commands, running through the snow with heavy bazookalike weapons on their shoulders, and lodging those death rays along the icy rims of the trenches.

The Rebel power generators near the gun towers began popping, buzzing, and crackling with deafening bursts of electrical power—enough to supply the vast underground complex. But above all this activity and noise a strange sound could be heard, an ominous thumping that was coming nearer and was beginning to shake the frozen ground. When it was close enough to attract the attention of an officer, he strained to see through the storm, looking for the source of the heavy, rhythmic pounding. Other men looked up from their work and saw what looked like a number of moving specks. Through the blizzard, the small dots seemed to be advancing at a slow yet steady pace, churning up clouds of snow as they moved toward the Rebel base.

The officer raised his electrobinoculars and focused on the approaching objects. There must have been a dozen of them resolutely advancing through the snow, looking like creatures out of some uncharted past. But they were machines, each of them stalking like enormous ungulates on four jointed legs.

Walkers!

With a shock of recognition, the officer identified the Empire's All Terrain Armored Transports. Each machine was formidably armed with cannons placed on its foreside like the horns of some prehistoric beast. Moving like mechanized pachyderms, the walkers emitted deadly fire from their turnstile guns and cannons.

The officer grabbed his comlink. "Rogue Leader . . . Incoming! Point Zero Three."

"Echo Station Five-Seven, we're on our way."

Even as Luke Skywalker replied, an explosion sprayed ice and snow around the officer and his terror-struck men. The walkers already had them within range. The troopers knew their job was to divert attention while the transport ships were launched, but none of the Rebel soldiers was prepared to die under the feet or weapons of these horrible machines.

Brilliant billows of orange and yellow flames exploded from the walker guns. Nervously the Rebel troopers aimed their weapons at the walkers, each soldier feeling icy, unseen fingers pierce his body.

Of the twelve snowspeeders, four took the lead, soaring at full throttle as they moved toward the enemy. One All Terrain Armored Transport machine fired, barely missing the banking craft. A burst of gunfire blew another speeder into a ball of flaming oblivion that lit up the sky.

Luke saw the explosion of his squadron's first casualty as he looked from his cockpit window. Angrily, Luke fired his ship's guns at a walker, only to receive a hail of Imperial fire power that shook his speeder in a barrage of flak.

Regaining control of his ship, Luke was joined by another snowspeeder, Rogue Three. They swarmed like insects around the relentlessly stomping walkers, as other speeders continued to exchange fire with the Imperial assault machines. Rogue Leader and Rogue Three flitted alongside the lead walker, then moved away from each other, both banking to the right.

Luke saw the horizon tilt as he maneuvered his speeder between the walker's jointed legs and soared out from under the monster machine. Bringing his speeder back to horizontal flight, the young commander contacted his companion ship. "Rogue Leader to Rogue Three."

"Copy, Rogue Leader," acknowledged Wedge, the pilot of Rogue Three.

"Wedge," Luke called into his comlink, "split your squad into pairs." Luke's snowspeeder then banked and turned, while Wedge's ship moved off in the opposite direction with another Rebel craft.

The walkers, firing all cannons, continued their march across the snow. Inside one of the assault machines two Imperial pilots had spotted the Rebel guns, conspicuous against the white field. The pilots began to maneuver the walker toward the guns when they noticed a lone snowspeeder making a reckless charge directly toward their main viewport, guns blazing. A huge explosion flashed outside the impenetrable window and dissipated as the snowspeeder, roaring through the smoke, disappeared overhead.

As Luke soared up and away from the walker, he looked back. That armor is too strong for blasters, he thought. There *must* be some other way of attacking these horrors; something other than fire power. For a moment Luke thought of some of the simple tactics a farm boy might employ against a wild beast. Then, turning his snowspeeder for yet another run against the walkers, he made a decision.

"Rogue group," he called into his comlink, "use your harpoons and tow cables. Go for the legs. It's our only hope of stopping them. Hobbie, are you still with me?"

The reassuring voice immediately responded. "Yes, sir."

"Well, stick close now."

As he leveled his ship, Luke was grimly determined to glide in tight formation with Hobbie. Together they veered, dropping nearer Hoth's surface.

In Luke's cockpit, his gunner, Dack, was jostled by the abrupt movement of the craft. Trying to keep his grip on the Rebel harpoon gun in his hand, he shouted, "Whoea! Luke, I can't seem to find my restraints."

Explosions rocked Luke's ship, tossing it about violently in the enveloping flak. Through the window he could see another walker that appeared to be unaffected by the full fire power of the Rebel attack speeders. This lumbering machine now became Luke's target as he flew, moving in a descending arc. The walker was firing directly at him, creating a wall of laser bolts and flak.

"Just hang on, Dack," he yelled over the explosions, "and get ready to fire that tow cable!"

Another great blast shook Luke's snowspeeder. He fought to regain control as the ship wobbled in its flight. Luke began to sweat profusely, despite the cold, as he desperately attempted to right his plunging ship. But the horizon still spun in front of him.

"Stand by, Dack. We're almost there. Are you okay?"

Dack didn't answer. Luke managed to turn and saw that Hobbie's speeder was maintaining its course next to him as they evaded the explosions bursting around them. He craned his head around and saw Dack, blood streaming from his forehead, slumped against the controls.

"Dack!"

On the ground, the gun towers near the Rebel power generators blasted away at the walking Imperial machines, but with no apparent effect. Imperial weapons bombarded the area all around them, blasting the snow skyward, almost blinding their human targets with the continuous onslaught. The officer who had first seen the incredible machines and fought alongside his men, was one of the first to be cut down by a walker's body-ripping rays. Troops rushed to his aid, but couldn't save him; too much of his blood had already spilled, making a scarlet stain against the snow.

More Rebel fire power blasted from one of the dishlike guns that had been erected near the power generators. Despite these tremendous explosions, the walkers continued to march. Another speeder made a heroic dive between a pair of the walkers, only to be caught by fire from one of the machines that exploded it into a great ball of rippling flames.

The surface explosions made the walls of the ice hangar tremble, causing deep cracks to spread.

Han Solo and Chewbacca were working frantically to complete their welding job. As they worked, it became obvious that the widening cracks would soon bring the entire ice ceiling smashing down upon them.

"First chance we get," Han said, "we're giving this crate a complete overhaul." But he knew that first he would have to get the *Millennium Falcon* out of this white hell.

Even as he and the Wookiee labored on the ship, enormous pieces of ice, broken loose by the explosions, came tumbling down throughout the underground base. Princess Leia moved quickly, trying to avoid the falling frozen chunks, as she sought shelter in the Rebel command center.

"I'm not sure we can protect two transports at a time," General Rieekan told her as she entered the chamber.

"It's risky," she answered, "but our holding action is faltering." Leia realized that the transport launchings were taking too much time and that the procedure had to be hastened.

Rieekan issued a command through his comlink. "Launch patrol, proceed with accelerated departures . . ."

As the general gave his order, Leia looked toward an aide and said, "Begin clearing the remaining ground staff." But she knew that their escape depended completely on Rebel success in the on-going battle above.

Inside the cold and cramped cockpit of the lead Imperial walker, General Veers moved between his snow-suited pilots. "What is the distance to the power generators?"

Without looking away from the control panel, one of the pilots replied, "Six-four-one."

Satisfied, General Veers reached for an electro-telescope and peered through the viewfinder to focus on the bullet-shaped power generators and the Rebel soldiers fighting to save them. Suddenly the walker began to rock violently under a barrage of Rebel gunfire. As he was propelled backward, Veers saw his pilots scrambling over the controls to keep the machine from toppling over.

The Rogue Three snowspeeder had just attacked the lead walker. Its pilot, Wedge, hooted with a loud Rebel shout of victory as he saw the damage his guns had caused.

Other snowspeeders passed Wedge, racing in the opposite direction. He steered his craft on a direct course toward another walking death machine. As he approached the monster, Wedge shouted to his gunner, "Activate harpoon!"

The gunner pressed the firing switch as his pilot daringly maneuvered their craft through the walker's legs. Immediately the harpoon whooshed from the rear of the speeder, a long length of cable unwinding behind it.

"Cable out!" the gunner yelled. "Let her go!"

Wedge saw the harpoon plunge into one of the metal legs, the cable still connected to his snowspeeder. He checked his controls, then brought the speeder around in front of the Imperial machine. Making an abrupt turn, Wedge guided his ship around one of the hind legs, the cable banding around it like a metallic lariat.

So far, thought Wedge, Luke's plan was working. Now all he had to do was fly his speeder around to the tail end of the walker. Wedge caught a glimpse of Rogue Leader as he carried out the maneuver.

"Cable out!" shouted the speeder's gunner again as Wedge flew their craft alongside the cable-entangled walker, close to the metal hull. Wedge's gunner depressed another switch and released the cable from the rear of the snowspeeder.

The speeder zoomed away and Wedge laughed as he looked down at the results of their efforts. The walker was awkwardly struggling to continue on its way, but the Rebel cable had completely entangled its legs. Finally it leaned to one side and crashed against the ground, its impact stirring up a cloud of ice and snow.

"Rogue Leader . . . One down, Luke," Wedge announced to the pilot of his companion speeder.

"I see it, Wedge," Commander Skywalker answered. "Good work."

In the trenches, Rebel troops cheered in triumph when they saw the assault machine topple. An officer leaped from his snow trench and signaled his men. Bolting out of the trench, he led his troopers in a boisterous charge against the fallen walker, reaching the great metallic hulk before a single Imperial soldier could pull himself free.

The Rebels were about to enter the walker when it suddenly exploded from within, hurtling great jagged chunks of torn metal at them, the impact of the blast flinging the stunned troops back against the snow.

Luke and Zev could see the destruction of the walker as they flew overhead, banking from right to left to avoid the flak bursting around them.

When they finally leveled off, their craft were shaken by explosions from the walkers' cannons.

"Steady, Rogue Two," Luke said, looking over at the snowspeeder flying parallel to his own ship. "Set harpoon. I'll cover for you."

But there was another explosion, this one damaging the front section of Zev's ship. The pilot could barely see through the engulfing cloud of smoke that fogged his windshield. He fought to keep his ship on a horizontal path, but more blasts by the enemy made it rock violently.

His view had become so obscured that it wasn't until Zev was directly in the line of fire that he saw the massive image of another Imperial walker. Rogue Two's pilot felt an instant of pain; then his snub-nosed craft, spewing smoke and hurtling on a collision course with the walker, suddenly erupted in flames amid a burst of cannon fire. Very little of Zev or his ship remained to hit the ground.

Luke saw the disintegration and was sickened by the loss of yet another friend. But he couldn't let himself dwell on his grief, especially now when so many other lives depended on his steady leadership.

He looked around desperately, then spoke into his comlink. "Wedge . . . Wedge . . . Rogue Three. Set your harpoon and follow me on the next pass."

As he spoke, Luke was hit hard by a terrific explosion that ripped through his speeder. He struggled with the controls in a futile attempt to keep the small craft under control. A chill of fear swept over him when he noticed the dense twisting funnel of black smoke pouring from his ship's aft section. He realized then that there was no way his damaged speeder could remain aloft. And, to make matters even worse, a walker loomed directly in his path.

Luke struggled with the controls as his ship plunged toward the ground, leaving a trail of smoke and flames behind. By then the heat in the cockpit was nearly unbearable. Flames were beginning to leap about inside the speeder and were coming uncomfortably close to Luke. He finally brought his ship down to skid and crash into the snow just a few meters away from one of the walking Imperial machines.

After impact, Luke struggled to pull himself from the cockpit and looked with horror at the looming figure of the approaching walker.

Gathering all his strength, Luke quickly squeezed himself from under the twisted metal of the control board and moved up against the top of his cockpit. Somehow he managed to open the hatch halfway and climbed out of the ship. With each elephantine step of the oncoming walker, the speeder shook violently. Luke had not realized just how enormous these four-legged horrors were until, unprotected by the shelter of his craft, he saw one up close.

Then he remembered Dack and returned to try and pull his friend's lifeless form from the wrecked speeder. But Luke had to give up. The body was too tightly wedged in the cockpit, and the walker was now almost upon him. Braving the flames, Luke reached into his speeder and grabbed the harpoon gun.

He gazed at the advancing mechanical behemoth and suddenly had an idea. He reached back inside the cockpit of the speeder and groped for a land mine attached to the ship's interior. With a great effort he stretched his fingers and firmly grasped the mine.

Luke leaped away from his vehicle just as the

towering machine lifted a massive foot and planted it firmly on the snowspeeder, crushing it flat.

Luke crouched underneath the walker, moving with it to avoid its slow steps. Raising his head, he felt the cold wind slap against his face as he studied the monster's vast underbelly.

As he ran along under the machine, Luke aimed his harpoon gun and fired. A powerful magnet attached to a long thin cable was ejected from the gun and firmly attached itself to the machine's underbelly.

Still running, Luke yanked on the cable, testing to make sure its strength was sufficient to sustain his weight. Then he attached the cable drum to the buckle of his utility belt, allowing its mechanism to pull him up off the ground. Now, dangling from the monster's underbelly, Luke could see the remaining walkers and two Rebel snowspeeders continuing the battle as they soared through fiery explosions.

He climbed up to the machine's hull where he had observed a small hatch. Quickly cutting it open with his laser sword, Luke pulled open the hatch, threw in the land mine, and made a rapid descent along the cable. As he reached the end, Luke dropped hard onto the snow and became unconscious; his inert body was nearly brushed by one of the walker's hind feet.

As the walker passed over and away from him, a muffled explosion tore at its insides. Suddenly the tremendous bulk of the mechanical beast exploded at the seams, machinery and pieces of hull flying in every direction. The Imperial assault machine crumbled into a smoking, motionless heap coming to rest upon what remained of its four stiltlike legs.

VI

THE Rebel command center, its walls and ceiling still shaking and cracking under the force of the battle on the surface, was attempting to operate amid the destruction. Pipes, torn apart by the blasting, belched sprays of scalding steam. The white floors were littered with broken pieces of machinery and chunks of ice were scattered everywhere. Except for the distant rumblings of laser fire, the command center was forebodingly quiet.

There were still Rebel personnel on duty, including Princess Leia, who watched the images on the few still-functioning console screens. She wanted to be certain that the last of the transport ships had slipped past the Imperial armada and were approaching their rendezvous point in space.

Han Solo rushed into the command center, dodging great sections of the ice ceiling that came plunging down at him. One great chunk was followed by an avalanche of ice that poured onto the floor near the entrance to the chamber. Undaunted, Han hurried to the control board where Leia stood beside See-Threepio.

"I heard the command center was hit." Han appeared concerned. "Are you all right?"

The princess nodded. She was surprised to see him there where the danger was severest.

"Come on," he urged before she could reply. "You've got to get to your ship."

Leia looked exhausted. She had been standing at the console viewscreens for hours and had participated in dispatching Rebel personnel to their posts. Taking her hand, Han led her from the chamber, with the protocol droid clacking after them.

As they left, Leia gave one final order to the controller. "Give the evacuation code signal . . . and get to the transport."

Then, as Leia, Han, and Threepio made their hasty exit from the command center, a voice blared from the public address speakers, echoing in the nearby deserted ice corridors. "Disengage, disengage! Begin retreat action!"

"Come on," Han urged, grimacing. "If you don't get there fast, your ship won't be able to take off."

The walls quaked even more violently than before. Ice chunks continued to fall throughout the underground base as the three hurried toward the transport ships. They had nearly reached the hangar where Leia's transport ship was waiting, ready for departure. But as they neared the corner they found the entrance to the hangar completely blocked by ice and snow.

Han knew they would have to find some other route to Leia's escape ship—and quickly. He began to lead them back down the corridor, careful to avoid falling ice, and snapped on his comlink as they hurried toward the ship. "Transport C One Seven!" he yelled into the small microphone. "We're coming! Hold on!"

They were close enough to the hangar to hear Leia's escape vessel preparing for lift-off from the Rebel ice base. If he could lead them safely just a few meters more, the princess would be safe and—

The chamber suddenly quaked with a terrible noise that thundered through the underground base. In an instant the entire ceiling had crashed down in front of them, creating a solid barrier of ice between them and the hangar docks. They stared in shock at the dense white mass.

"We're cut off," Han yelled into his comlink, knowing that if the transport were to make good its escape there could be no time wasted in melting down or blasting through the barricade. "You'll have to take off without Princess Organa." He turned to her. "If we're lucky we can still make it to the *Falcon*."

The princess and See-Threepio followed as Han dashed toward another chamber, hoping that the *Millennium Falcon* and his Wookiee copilot had not already been buried under an avalanche of ice.

Looking out across the white battlefield, the Rebel officer watched the remaining snowspeeders whisking through the air and the last of the Imperial vehicles as they passed the wreckage of the exploded walker. He flipped on his comlink and heard the order to retreat: "Disengage, disengage. Begin retreat action." As he signaled his men to move back inside the ice cavern, he noticed that the lead walker was still treading heavily in the direction of the power generators.

In the cockpit of that assault machine, General Veers stepped close to the port. From this position he could clearly see the target below. He studied the crackling power generators and observed the Rebel troops defending them.

"Point-three-point-three-point-five . . . coming within range, sir," reported his pilot.

The general turned to his assault officer. "All troops will debark for ground assault," Veers said. "Prepare to target the main generator."

The lead walker, flanked by two of the hulking machines, lurched forward, its guns blazing to scatter the retreating Rebel troops.

As more laser fire came from the oncoming walkers, Rebel bodies and parts of Rebel bodies were flung through the air. Many of the soldiers who had managed to avoid the obliterating laser beams were crushed into unrecognizable pulp beneath the walkers' stomping feet. The air was charged with the stink of blood and burning flesh, and thundering with the explosive noises of battle.

As they fled, the few surviving Rebel soldiers glimpsed a lone snowspeeder as it retreated in the distance, a black trail of smoke escaping its burning hull.

Although the smoke rising from his crippled speeder obstructed his view, Hobbie could still see some of the carnage that raged on the ground. His wounds from a walker's laser fire made it torture even to move, let alone operate the controls of his craft. But if he could manage to work them just long enough to return to the base, he might be able to find a medical robot and . . .

No, he doubted he would survive even that long. He was dying—of that he was now certain—and the men in the trench would soon be dead, too, unless something were done to save them.

General Veers, proudly transmitting his report to Imperial headquarters, was totally unaware of Rogue Four's approach. "Yes, Lord Vader, I've reached the main power generators. The shield will be down in moments. You may commence your landing."

As he ended his transmission, General Veers reached for the electrorangefinder and looked through the eyepiece to line up the main power generators. Electronic crosshairs aligned according to the information from the walker's computers. Then suddenly the readouts on the small monitor screens mysteriously vanished.

Confounded, General Veers moved away from the eyepiece of the electrorangefinder and turned instinctively toward a cockpit window. He flinched in terror at seeing a smoking projectile heading on a direct course toward his walker's cockpit.

The other pilots also saw the hurtling speeder, and knew that there was no time to turn the massive assault machine. "He's going to—" one of the pilots began.

At that instant, Hobbie's burning ship crashed through the walker cockpit like a manned bomb, its fuel igniting into a cascade of flame and debris. For a second there were human screams, then fragments, and the entire machine crashed to the ground.

Perhaps it was the sound of this nearby blast that jarred Luke Skywalker back to consciousness. Dazed, he slowly lifted his head from the snow. He felt very weak and was achingly stiff with cold. The thought crossed his mind that frostbite might already have damaged his tissues. He hoped not; he had no desire to spend any more time in that sticky bacta fluid.

He tried to stand, but fell back against the snow, hoping he would not be spotted by any of the walker pilots. His comlink whistled, and somehow he found the strength to flick on its receiver.

"Forward units' withdrawal complete," the broadcast voice reported.

Withdrawal? Luke thought a moment. Then Leia and the others must have escaped! Luke suddenly felt that all the fighting and the deaths of loyal Rebel personnel had not been for nothing. A warmth rushed through his body, and he gathered his strength to rise and begin making the long trek back toward a distant formation of ice.

Another explosion rocked the Rebel hangar deck, cracking the ceiling and almost burying the docked *Millennium Falcon* in a mound of ice. At any moment the entire ceiling might cave in. The only safe place in the hangar seemed to be underneath the ship itself where Chewbacca was impatiently awaiting the return of his captain. The Wookiee had begun to worry. If Han did not return soon, the *Falcon* would surely be buried in a tomb of ice. But loyalty to his partner kept Chewie from taking off in the freighter alone.

As the hangar started to tremble more violently, Chewbacca detected movement in the adjoining chamber. Throwing back his head, the shaggy giant filled the hangar with his loudest roar as he saw Han Solo climb over hills of ice and snow and enter the chamber, followed closely by Princess Leia and an obviously nervous See-Threepio.

Not far from the hangar, Imperial stormtroopers, their faces shielded by white helmets and white snowscreens, had begun moving down deserted corridors. With them strode their leader, the dark-robed figure who surveyed the shambles that had been the Rebel base at Hoth. Darth Vader's black image stood out starkly against the white walls, ceiling, and floor. As he moved through the white catacombs, he regally stepped aside to avoid a falling section of the ice ceiling. Then he continued on his way with such quick strides that his troops had to hurry to keep up.

A low whine, rising in pitch, began to issue from the saucer-shaped freighter. Han Solo stood at the controls in the *Millennium Falcon*'s cockpit, at last feeling at home. He quickly flipped one switch after another, expecting to see the board flash its familiar mosaic of light; but only some of the lights were working.

Chewbacca had also noticed something amiss and barked with concern as Leia examined a gauge that seemed to be malfunctioning.

"How's that, Chewie?" asked Han anxiously.

The Wookiee's bark was distinctly negative.

"Would it help if I got out and pushed?" snapped Princess Leia, who was beginning to wonder if it were the Corellian's spit that held the ship together.

"Don't worry, Your Holiness. I'll get it started."

See-Threepio clanked into the hold and, gesturing, tried to get Han's attention. "Sir," the robot volunteered, "I was wondering if I might—" But his scanners read the scowl on the face staring at him. "It can wait," he concluded.

Imperial stormtroopers, accompanied by the rapidly moving Darth Vader, thundered through the ice corridors of the Rebel base. Their pace quickened as they rushed in the direction of the low whine coming from the ion engines. Vader's body tensed slightly as, entering the hangar, he perceived the familiar saucer-shaped form of the *Millennium Falcon.*

Within the battered freighter ship, Han Solo and Chewbacca were trying desperately to get the craft moving.

"This bucket of bolts is never going to get us past that blockade," Princess Leia complained.

Han pretended that he didn't hear her. Instead, he checked the *Falcon*'s controls and struggled to keep his patience even though his companion had so obviously lost hers. He flipped switches on the control console, ignoring the princess's look of disdain. Clearly, she doubted that this assemblage of spare parts and welded hunks of scrap metal would hold together even if they *did* manage to get beyond the blockade.

Han pushed a button on the intercom. "Chewie . . . come on!" Then, winking at Leia, he said, "This baby's still got a few surprises left in her."

"I'll be surprised if we start moving."

Before Han could make a carefully honed retort, the *Falcon* was jolted by a blast of Imperial laser fire that flashed outside the cockpit window. They could all see the squad of Imperial stormtroopers rushing with drawn weapons into the far end of the ice hangar. Han knew that the *Falcon*'s dented hull might resist the force of those hand weapons, but would be destroyed by the more powerful bazooka-shaped weapon that two of the Imperial troopers were hurriedly setting up.

"Chewie!" Han yelled as he quickly strapped himself into his pilot's chair. Meanwhile, a somewhat subdued young woman seated herself in the navigator's chair.

Outside the *Millennium Falcon,* stormtroopers worked with military efficiency to set up their enormous gun. Behind them the hangar doors began to open. One of the *Falcon*'s powerful laser weapons appeared from the hull and swung about, aiming directly at the stormtroopers.

Han moved urgently to block the Imperial soldiers' efforts. Without hesitation he released a deadly blast from the powerful laser weapon he had aimed at the stormtroopers. The explosion scattered their armored bodies all over the hangar.

Chewbacca dashed into the cockpit.

"We'll just have to switch over," Han announced, "and hope for the best."

The Wookiee hurled his hairy bulk into the copilot's seat as yet another laser blast erupted outside the window next to him. He yelled indignantly, then yanked back on the controls to bring the welcome roar of engine fire from deep inside the *Falcon*.

The Corellian grinned at the princess, a gleeful I-told-you-so gleam in his eyes.

"Someday," she said with mild disgust, "you're going to be wrong, and I just hope I'm there to see it."

Han just smiled, then turned to his copilot. "Punch it!" he shouted.

The huge freighter's engines roared. And everything behind the craft instantly melted in the fiery exhaust billowing from its tailpiece. Chewbacca furiously worked the controls, watching out of the corner of his eyes the ice walls rushing past as the freighter blasted away.

At the last moment, just before takeoff, Han caught a glimpse of additional stormtroopers running into the hangar. In their wake strode a foreboding giant clad entirely in black. Then there was only the blur and the beckoning of billions of stars.

As the *Millennium Falcon* soared from the hangar, its flight was detected by Commander Luke Skywalker, who turned to smile at Wedge and his gunner. "At least Han got away." The three then trudged along to their waiting X-wing fighter ships. When they finally reached them, they shook hands and moved off toward their separate vehicles.

"Good luck, Luke," Wedge said as they parted. "See you at the rendezvous."

Luke waved and began to walk toward his X-wing. Standing there amid the mountains of ice and snow, he was overcome by a surge of loneliness. He felt desperately alone now that even Han was gone. Worse than that, Princess Leia was also somewhere else; she might just as well be an entire universe away . . .

Then out of nowhere a familiar whistle greeted Luke.

"Artoo!" he exclaimed. "Is that you?"

Sitting snugly in the socket that had been installed for these helpful R2 units was the little barrel-shaped droid, his head peeking from the top of the ship. Artoo had scanned the approaching figure and had whistled with relief when his computers informed him it was Luke. The young commander was equally relieved to reencounter the robot that had accompanied him on so many of his previous adventures.

As he climbed into the cockpit and seated himself behind the controls, Luke could hear the sound of Wedge's fighter roaring into the sky toward the Rebel rendezvous point. "Activate the power and stop worrying. We'll soon be airborne," Luke said in response to Artoo's nervous beeping.

His was the last Rebel ship to abandon what

had, for a very brief time, been a secret outpost in the revolution against the tyranny of the Empire.

Darth Vader, a raven specter, quickly strode through the ruins of the Rebel ice fortress, forcing his accompanying men into a brisk jog to keep up. As they moved through the corridors, Admiral Piett rushed up to overtake his master.

"Seventeen ships destroyed," he reported to the Dark Lord. "We don't know how many got away."

Without turning his head, Vader snarled through his mask, "The *Millennium Falcon*?"

Piett paused a moment before replying. He would have preferred to avoid *that* issue. "Our tracking scanners are on it now," he responded a bit fearfully.

Vader turned to face the admiral, his towering figure looming over the frightened officer. Piett felt a chill course through his veins, and when the Dark Lord spoke again his voice conveyed an image of the dreadful fate that would be inflicted if his commands were not executed.

"I want that ship," he hissed.

The ice planet was rapidly shrinking to a point of dim light as the *Millennium Falcon* sped into space. Soon that planet seemed nothing more than one of the billions of light specks scattered throughout the black void.

But the *Falcon* was not alone in its escape into deep space. Rather, it was followed by an Imperial fleet that included the *Avenger* Star Destroyer and a half-dozen TIE fighters. The fighters moved ahead of the huge, slower-moving Destroyer, and closed in on the fleeing *Millennium Falcon*.

Chewbacca howled over the roar of the *Falcon's*

engines. The ship was beginning to lurch with the buffeting flak blasted at it by the fighters.

"I know, I know, I see them," Han shouted. It was taking everything he had to maintain control of the ship.

"See what?" Leia asked.

Han pointed out the window at two very bright objects.

"Two more Star Destroyers, and they're heading right at us."

"I'm glad you said there was going to be no problem," she commented with more than a touch of sarcasm, "or I'd be worried."

The ship rocked under the steady fire from the TIE fighters, making it difficult for Threepio to maintain his balance as he returned to the cockpit. His metal skin bumped and banged against the walls as he approached Han. "Sir," he began tentatively, "I was wondering . . ."

Han Solo shot him a threatening glance. "Either shut up or shut down," Han warned the robot, who immediately did the former.

Still struggling with the controls to keep the *Millennium Falcon* on course, the pilot turned to the Wookiee. "Chewie, how's the deflector shield holding up?"

The copilot adjusted an overhead switch and barked a reply that Solo interpreted as positive.

"Good," said Han. "At sublight, they may be faster, but we can still out-maneuver them. Hold on!" Suddenly the Corellian shifted his ship's course.

The two Imperial Star Destroyers had come almost within firing range of the *Falcon* as they loomed ahead; the pursuing TIE fighters and the *Avenger* were also dangerously close. Han felt he had no choice but to take the *Falcon* into a ninety-degree dive.

Leia and Chewbacca felt their stomachs leap into their throats as the *Falcon* executed its steep dive. Poor Threepio quickly had to alter his inner mechanisms if he wanted to remain on his metallic feet.

Han realized that his crew might think he was some kind of lunatic star jockey, pushing his ship on this madman's course. But he had a strategy in mind. With the *Falcon* no longer between them, the two Star Destroyers were now on a direct collision course with the *Avenger*. All he had to do was sit back and watch.

Alarms blared through the interiors of all three Star Destroyers. These ponderously massive ships could not respond quickly enough to such emergencies. Sluggishly one of the Destroyers began to move to the left in its effort to avoid collision with the *Avenger*. Unfortunately, as it veered, it brushed its companion ship, violently shaking up both spaceborne fortresses. The damaged Destroyers began to drift through space, while the *Avenger* continued in pursuit of the *Millennium Falcon* and its obviously insane pilot.

Two down, Han thought. But there was still a quartet of TIE fighters tailing the *Falcon,* blasting at its stern with full laser fire, but Han thought he could outstrip them. The ship was buffeted violently by the fighters' laser blasts, forcing Leia to hold on in a desperate attempt to keep her seat.

"That slowed them down a bit!" Han exulted. "Chewie, stand by to make the jump to lightspeed." There was not a moment to waste—the laser attack was intense now, and the TIE fighters were almost on top of them.

"They're very close," Leia warned, finally able to speak.

Han looked at her with a wicked glint in his eyes. "Oh, yeah? Watch this."

He threw the hyperspace throttle forward, desperate to escape, but also eager to impress the princess with both his own cleverness and his ship's fantastic power. Nothing happened! The stars that should by then have been mere blurs of light were still. Something was definitely wrong.

"Watch what?" Leia asked impatiently.

Instead of responding, Han worked the light-speed controls a second time. Again, nothing. "I think we're in trouble," he muttered. His throat tightened. He knew "trouble" was a gross under-statement.

"If I may say so, sir," Threepio volunteered, "I noticed earlier that the entire main para-light system seemed to have been damaged."

Chewbacca threw back his head and let out a loud and miserable wail.

"We're in trouble!" Han repeated.

All around them, the laser attack had increased violently. The *Millennium Falcon* could only continue at its maximum sublight velocity as it moved deeper into space, closely followed by a swarm of TIE fighters and one gigantic Imperial Star De-stroyer.

VII

THE double sets of wings on Luke Skywalker's X-wing fighter were pulled together to form one wing as the small, sleek craft streaked away from the planet of snow and ice.

During his flight, the young commander had time to reflect on the events of the past few days. He now had time to ponder the enigmatic words of the ghostly Ben Kenobi and think about his friendship with Han Solo, and also consider his tenuous relationship with Leia Organa. As he thought of the people he cared most about, he arrived at a sudden decision. Gazing back one last time at the small icy planet, he told himself there was no longer any turning back.

Luke flipped a number of switches on his control board and took the X-wing into a steep turn. He watched the heavens shift as he rocketed off in a new direction, flying at top velocity. He was bringing his craft back onto an even course when Artoo, still snug in his specially designed socket, began to whistle and beep.

The miniature computer installed in Luke's ship for translating the droid's language flashed the small droid's message onto a control panel viewscreen.

"There's nothing wrong, Artoo," Luke replied

after reading the translation. "I'm just setting a new course."

The small droid beeped excitedly, and Luke turned to read the updated printout on the viewscreen.

"No," Luke replied, "we're not going to regroup with the others."

This news startled Artoo, who immediately emitted a series of galvanic noises.

"We're going to the Dagobah system," answered Luke.

Again the robot beeped, calculating the amount of fuel carried by the X-wing.

"We have enough power."

Artoo gave vent to a longer, singsong series of toots and whistles.

"They don't need us there," said Luke to the droid's question about the planned Rebel rendezvous.

Artoo then gently beeped a reminder about Princess Leia's order. Exasperated, the young pilot exclaimed, "I'm countermanding that order! Now, be still."

The little droid fell silent. Luke was, after all, a commander in the Rebel Alliance and, as such, could countermand orders. He was making a few minor adjustments on the controls when Artoo chirped up again.

"Yes, Artoo," sighed Luke.

This time the droid made a series of soft noises, selecting each beep and whistle carefully. He did not want to annoy Luke, but the findings on his computer were important enough to report.

"Yes, Artoo, I know the Dagobah system doesn't appear on any of our navigational charts. But don't worry. It's there."

Another worried beep from the R2 unit.

"I'm very sure," the youth said, trying to reassure his mechanical companion. "Trust me."

Whether or not Artoo did trust the human being at the X-wing's controls, he only vented a meek little sigh. For a moment he was completely silent, as if thinking. Then he beeped again.

"Yes, Artoo?"

This communication from the robot was even more carefully put forth than before—one might even call the whistle-sentences tactful. It seemed Artoo had no intention of offending the human to whom he had entrusted himself. But wasn't it possible, the robot calculated, that the human's brain was slightly malfunctioning? After all, he had lain a long time in the snowdrifts of Hoth. Or, another possibility computed by Artoo, perhaps the Wampa Ice Creature had struck him more seriously than Too-One bee had diagnosed? . . .

"No," Luke answered, "no headache. I feel fine. Why?"

Artoo's chirp was coyly innocent.

"No dizziness, no drowsiness. Even the scars are gone."

The next whistle rose questioningly in pitch.

"No, that's all right, Artoo. I'd rather keep it on manual control for a while."

Then the stout robot delivered a final whimper that sounded to Luke like a noise of defeat. Luke was amused by the droid's concern for his health. "Trust me, Artoo," Luke said with a gentle smile. "I know where I'm going and I'll get us there safely. It's not far."

Han Solo was desperate now. The *Falcon* had still not been able to shrug off the four TIE fighters or the enormous Star Destroyer that pursued it.

Solo raced down to the ship's hold and began to work frantically on repairing the malfunctioning hyperdrive unit. It was all but impossible to carry out the delicate repair work necessary while the *Falcon* shook with each blast of flak from the fighters.

Han snapped orders at his copilot, who checked the mechanisms as he was commanded. "Horizontal booster."

The Wookiee barked. It looked fine to him.

"Alluvial damper."

Another bark. That part was also in place.

"Chewie, get me the hydrospanners."

Chewbacca rushed over to the pit with the tools. Han grabbed the spanners, then paused and looked at his faithful Wookiee friend.

"I don't know how we're going to get out of this one," he confided.

Just then a resounding *thump* hit the *Falcon*'s side, making the ship pitch and turn radically.

Chewbacca barked anxiously.

Han braced himself at the impact, the hydrospanners flew from his hand. When he managed to regain his balance, he shouted at Chewbacca over the noise, "That was no laser blast! Something hit us!"

"Han . . . Han . . ." Princess Leia called to him from the cockpit. She was frantic. "Get up here!"

Like a shot, he lurched out of the hold and raced back to the cockpit with Chewbacca. They were stunned by what they saw through the windows.

"Asteroids!"

Enormous chunks of flying rock hurtled through space as far as they could see. As if those damn Imperial pursuit ships weren't trouble enough!

Han instantly returned to his pilot's seat, once more taking over the *Falcon*'s controls. His copilot settled himself back into his own seat just as a particularly large asteroid sped by the prow of the ship.

Han felt he had to stay as calm as possible; otherwise they might not last more than a few moments. "Chewie," he ordered, "set two-seven-one."

Leia gasped. She knew what Han's order meant and was stunned by so reckless a plan. "You're not thinking of heading into the asteroid field?" she asked, hoping she had misunderstood his command.

"Don't worry, they won't follow us through this!" he shouted with glee.

"If I might remind you, sir," Threepio offered, trying to be a rational influence, "the probability of successfully navigating through an asteroid field is approximately two thousand four hundred and sixty-seven to one."

No one seemed to hear him.

Princess Leia scowled. "You don't have to do this to impress me," she said, as the *Falcon* was pummeled hard by another asteroid.

Han was enjoying himself enormously and chose to ignore her insinuations. "Hang on, sweetheart," he laughed, grasping the controls more tightly. "We're gonna do some *flyin'*."

Leia winced and, resigned, buckled herself firmly into her seat.

See-Threepio, still muttering calculations, shut down his synthesized human voice when the Wookiee turned and growled at him.

But Han concentrated only on carrying out his plan. He knew it would work; it had to—there was no other choice. Flying more on instinct than on instruments, he steered his ship through the relentless rain of stone. Glancing quickly at his scanner screens, he saw that the TIE fighters and the *Avenger*s had not yet abandoned the chase. It would be an Imperial funeral, he thought, as he maneuvered the *Falcon* through the asteroid hail.

He looked at another viewscreen and smiled as it showed a collision between an asteroid and a TIE fighter. The explosion registered on the screen with a burst of light. No survivors in *that* one, Han thought.

The TIE fighter pilots chasing the *Falcon* were among the best in the Empire. But they couldn't compete with Han Solo. Either they weren't good enough, or they weren't crazy enough. Only a lunatic would have plunged his ship into a suicidal journey through these asteroids. Crazy or not, these pilots had no choice but to follow in hot pursuit. They undoubtedly would be better off perishing in this bombardment of rocks than reporting failure to their dark master.

The greatest of all the Imperial Star Destroyers regally moved out of Hoth's orbit. It was flanked by two other Star Destroyers and the entire group was accompanied by a protective squadron of smaller warships. In the central Destroyer, Admiral Piett stood outside Darth Vader's private meditation chamber. The upper jaw slowly opened until Piett was able to glimpse his robed master standing in the shadows. "My lord," Piett said with reverence.

"Come in, Admiral."

Admiral Piett felt great awe as he stepped into

the dimly lit room and approached the Dark Lord of the Sith. His master stood silhouetted so that Piett could just barely make out the lines of a set of mechanical appendages as they retracted a respirator tube from Vader's head. He shuddered when he realized that he might be the first ever to have seen his master unmasked.

The sight was horrifying. Vader, his back turned to Piett, was entirely clothed in black; but above his studded black neck band gleamed his naked head. Though the admiral tried to avert his eyes, morbid fascination forced him to look at that hairless, skull-like head. It was covered with a maze of thick scar tissue that twisted around against Vader's corpse-pale skin. The thought crossed Piett's mind that there might be a heavy price for viewing what no one else had seen. Just then, the robot hands grasped the black helmet and gently lowered it over the Dark Lord's head.

His helmet back in place, Darth Vader turned to hear his admiral's report.

"Our pursuit ships have sighted the *Millennium Falcon,* my lord. It has entered an asteroid field."

"Asteroids don't concern me, Admiral," Vader said as he slowly clenched his fist. "I want that ship, not excuses. How long until you will have Skywalker and the others in the *Millennium Falcon?*"

"Soon, Lord Vader," the admiral answered, trembling in fear.

"Yes, Admiral . . ." Darth Vader said slowly, ". . . soon."

Two gigantic asteroids hurtled toward the *Millennium Falcon.* Its pilot quickly made a daring banking maneuver that brought it skirring out of the path of those two asteroids, nearly to collide with a third.

As the *Falcon* darted in and out of the asteroid field, it was followed closely by three Imperial TIE fighters that veered through the rocks in hot pursuit. Suddenly one of the three was fatally scraped by a shapeless chunk of rock and spun off in another direction, hopelessly out of control. The other two TIE fighters continued their chase, accompanied by the Star Destroyer *Avenger,* which was blasting speeding asteroids in its path.

Han Solo glimpsed the pursuing ships through the windows of his cockpit as he spun his craft around, speeding under yet another oncoming asteroid, then bringing the freighter back to its right-side-up position. But the *Millennium Falcon* was not yet out of danger. Asteroids were still streaking past the freighter. A small one bounced off the ship with a loud, reverberating *clang,* terrifying Chewbacca and causing See-Threepio to cover his eye lenses with a bronzed hand.

Han glanced at Leia and saw that she was sitting stone-faced as she stared at the swarm of asteroids. It looked to him as if she wished she were thousands of miles away.

"Well," he remarked, "you said you wanted to be around when I was wrong."

She didn't look at him. "I take it back."

"That Star Destroyer is slowing down," Han announced, checking his computer readings.

"Good," she replied shortly.

The view outside the cockpit was still thick with racing asteroids. "We're going to get pulverized if we stay out here much longer," he observed.

"I'm against that," Leia remarked dryly.

"We've got to get out of this shower."

"That makes sense."

"I'm going to get in closer to one of the big ones," Han added.

That did *not* make sense.

"Closer!" Threepio exclaimed, throwing up his metal arms. His artificial brain could scarcely register what his auditory sensors had just perceived.

"Closer!" Leia repeated in disbelief.

Chewbacca stared at his pilot in amazement and barked.

None of the three could understand why their captain, who had risked his life to save them all, would now try to get them killed! Making a few simple adjustments on the cockpit controls, Han swerved the *Millennium Falcon* between a few large asteroids, then aimed the craft directly at one the size of a moon.

A flashing shower of smaller rocks exploded against the enormous asteroid's craggy surface as the *Millennium Falcon,* with the Emperor's TIE fighters still in pursuit, flew directly above the asteroid. It was like skimming over the surface of a small planet, barren and devoid of all life.

With expert precision, Han Solo steered his ship toward still another giant asteroid, the largest one they had yet encountered. Summoning all the skill that had made his reputation known throughout the galaxy, he maneuvered the *Falcon* so that the only object between it and the TIE fighters was the deadly floating rock.

There was only a brief, brilliant flare of light, then nothing. The shattered remains of the two TIE fighters drifted away into the darkness and the tremendous asteroid—undeflected in its course— continued on its way.

Han felt an inner glow as bright as the spectacle

that had just lighted up the view. He smiled to himself in quiet triumph.

Then he noticed an image on the main scope of his control console and nudged his hairy copilot. "There." Han pointed to the image. "Chewie, get a reading on that. Looks pretty good."

"What is it?" Leia asked.

The *Falcon*'s pilot ignored her question. "That should do nicely," he said.

As they flew near the asteroid's surface, Han looked down at the craggy terrain, his eye caught by a shadowy area that looked like a crater of mammoth proportions. He lowered the *Falcon* to surface level and flew it directly into the crater, its bowllike walls suddenly rising up around his ship.

And still two TIE fighters chased after him, firing their laser cannons and attempting to mimic his every maneuver.

Han Solo knew he had to be trickier and more daring if he was to lose the deadly pursuit ships. Spotting a narrow chasm through his windscreen, he banked the *Millennium Falcon* to one side. The ship soared sideways through the high-walled rocky trench.

Unexpectedly the two TIE fighters followed. One of them even sparked as it grazed the walls with its metal hull.

Twisting, banking, and turning his ship, Han pressed through the narrow gorge. From behind, the black sky flared as the two TIE fighters crashed against one another, then exploded against the rocky ground.

Han reduced his speed. He still wasn't safe from the Imperial hunters. Searching about the canyon, he spotted something dark, a gaping cave mouth at the very bottom of the crater, large enough to hold the *Millennium Falcon*—perhaps. If not, he and his crew would know soon enough.

Slowing his ship, Han coursed into the cave entrance and through a large tunnel, which he hoped would make the ideal hiding place. He took a deep breath as his ship was promptly devoured by the cave's shadows.

A tiny X-wing was approaching the atmosphere of the Dagobah planet.

As he neared the planet, Luke Skywalker was able to glimpse a portion of its curved surface through a heavy cover of thick clouds. The planet was uncharted and virtually unknown. Somehow Luke had made his way there, though he wasn't certain whether it was his hand alone that had guided his ship into this unexplored sector of space.

Artoo-Detoo, riding in the back of Luke's X-wing, scanned the passing stars, then addressed his remarks to Luke via the computer scope.

Luke read the viewscreen interpreter. "Yes, that's Dagobah, Artoo," he answered the little robot, then glanced out the cockpit window as the fighter ship began to descend toward the planet's surface. "Looks a little grim, doesn't it?"

Artoo beeped, attempting for one last time to get his master back on a more sensible course.

"No," Luke replied, "I don't want to change my mind about this." He checked the ship's monitors and began to feel a bit nervous. "I'm not picking up any cities or technology. Massive life-form readings, though. There's something alive down there."

Artoo was worried, too, and that was translated as an apprehensive inquiry.

"Yes, I'm sure it's perfectly safe for droids. Will

you take it easy?" Luke was beginning to get annoyed. "We'll just have to see what happens."

He heard a pathetic electronic whimper from the rear of the cockpit.

"Don't worry!"

The X-wing sailed through the twilight halo separating pitch black space from the planet's surface. Luke took a deep breath, then plunged his craft into the white blanket of mists.

He couldn't see a thing. His vision was entirely obstructed by the dense whiteness pressing against the canopy windows of his ship. His only choice was to control his X-wing solely by instruments. But the scopes weren't registering anything, even as Luke flew ever nearer to the planet. Desperately he worked his controls, no longer able to discern even so much as his altitude.

When an alarm began to buzz, Artoo joined its clarion call with his own frantic series of whistles and beeps.

"I know, I know!" Luke shouted, still fighting the controls of his ship. "All the scopes are dead! I can't see a thing. Hang on, I'm going to start the landing cycle. Let's just hope there's something underneath us."

Artoo squealed again, but his sounds were effectively drowned by the ear-splitting blast of the X-wing's retrorockets. Luke felt his stomach plunge as the ship began to drop rapidly. He braced against his pilot's seat, steeling himself for any possible impact. Then the ship lunged and Luke heard an awful sound as if the limbs of trees were being snapped off by his speeding craft.

When the X-wing finally screeched to a halt, it was with a tremendous jolt that nearly flung its pilot through the cockpit window. Certain, at last, that he was on the ground, Luke slumped back in his chair and sighed with relief. He then pulled a switch that lifted his ship's canopy. When he raised his head outside the ship to get his first look at the alien world, Luke Skywalker gasped.

The X-wing was completely surrounded by mists, its bright landing lights not illuminating more than a few feet in front of it. Luke's eyes gradually began to grow accustomed to the gloom all around him so that he could just barely see the twisted trunks and roots of grotesque-looking trees. He pulled himself out of the cockpit as Artoo detached his stout body from its cubbyhole plug.

"Artoo," Luke said, "you stay put while I look around."

The enormous gray trees had gnarled and intertwining roots that rose far above Luke before they joined to form trunks. He tilted back his head and could see the branches, high above, that seemed to form a canopy with the low-hanging clouds. Luke cautiously climbed out onto the long nose of his ship and saw that he had crash-landed in a small, fog-shrouded body of water.

Artoo emitted a short beep—then there was a loud splash, followed by silence. Luke turned just in time to glimpse the droid's domed topside as it disappeared beneath the water's foggy surface.

"Artoo! Artoo!" Luke called. He kneeled down on the smooth hull of the ship and leaned forward, anxiously searching for his mechanical friend.

But the black waters were serene, revealing not a sign of the little R2 unit. Luke could not tell how deep this still, murky pond might be; but it looked *extremely* deep. He was suddenly gripped by the realization that he might never see his droid friend again. Just then, a tiny periscope broke through the surface of the water and Luke could hear a faint gurgling beep.

What a relief! Luke thought, as he watched the periscope make its way toward shore. He ran along the nose of his X-wing fighter, and when the shore line was less than three meters away, the young commander jumped into the water and scrambled up the shore. He looked back and saw that Artoo was still making his way toward the beach.

"Hurry, Artoo!" Luke shouted.

Whatever it was that suddenly moved through the water behind Artoo moved too quickly and was too obscured by the mist for Luke to clearly identify it. All he could see was a massive dark form. This creature rose up for a moment, then dove beneath the surface, making a loud bang against the little droid's metal hull. Luke heard the robot's pathetic electronic scream for help. Then, nothing . . .

Luke stood there, horror-struck, as he continued to stare at the black waters, still as death itself. As he watched, a few tell-tale bubbles began to erupt at the surface. Luke's heart began to pound in fear as he realized he was standing too near the pool. But before he could move, the runt-size robot was spit out by the thing lurking beneath the black surface. Artoo made a graceful arc through the air and came crashing down onto a soft patch of gray moss.

"Artoo," Luke yelled, running to him, "are you okay?" Luke was grateful that the shadowy swamp lurker apparently found metal droids neither palatable nor digestible.

Feebly the robot replied with a series of faint whistles and beeps.

"If you're saying coming here was a bad idea,

I'm beginning to agree with you," Luke admitted, looking around at their dismal surroundings. At least, he thought, there was human companionship on the ice world. Here, except for Artoo, there seemed to be nothing but this murky bog—and creatures, as yet unseen, that might lurk in the falling darkness.

Dusk was quickly approaching. Luke shivered in the thickening fog that closed in on him like something alive. He helped Artoo-Detoo back onto his feet, then wiped away the swamp muck that covered the droid's cylindrical body. As he worked, Luke heard eerie and inhuman cries that emanated from the distant jungle and shuddered as he imagined the beasts that might be making them.

By the time he finished cleaning off Artoo, Luke observed that the sky had grown noticeably darker. Shadows loomed ominously all around him and the distant cries didn't seem quite so far away anymore. He and Artoo glanced around at the spooky swamp-jungle surrounding them, then huddled a bit closer. Suddenly, Luke noticed a pair of tiny but vicious eyes winking at them through the shadowy underbrush, then vanishing with a scutter of diminutive feet.

He hesitated to doubt the advice of Ben Kenobi, but now he was beginning to wonder if that robed specter had somehow made a mistake leading him to this planet with its mysterious Jedi teacher.

He looked over at his X-wing and groaned when he saw that the entire bottom section was completely submerged in the dark waters. "How are we going to get that thing flying again?" The whole set of circumstances seemed hopeless and somewhat ridiculous. "What are we doing here?" he moaned.

It was beyond the computerized abilities of Artoo to provide an answer for either of those questions, but he made a little comforting beep anyway.

"It's like part of a dream," Luke said. He shook his head, feeling cold and frightened. "Or maybe I'm going crazy."

At least, he knew for certain, he couldn't have gotten himself into a crazier situation.

VIII

DARTH Vader looked like a great silent god as he stood on the main control deck of his mammoth Star Destroyer.

He was staring through the large rectangular window above the deck at the raging field of asteroids that was pelting his ship as it glided through space. Hundreds of rocks streaked past the windows. Some collided with one another and exploded in brilliant displays of vivid light.

As Vader watched, one of his smaller ships disintegrated under the impact of an enormous asteroid. Seemingly unmoved, he turned to look at a series of twenty holographic images. These twenty holograms re-created in three dimensions the features of twenty Imperial battleship commanders. The image of the commander whose ship had just been obliterated was fading rapidly, almost as quickly as the glowing particles of his exploded ship were being flung to oblivion.

Admiral Piett and an aide quietly moved to stand behind their black-garbed master as he turned to an image in the center of the twenty holograms which was continually interrupted by static and faded in and out as Captain Needa of the Star Destroyer *Avenger* made his report. His first words had already been drowned by static.

". . . which was the last time they appeared in any of our scopes," Captain Needa continued, "Considering the amount of damage we've sustained, they also must have been destroyed."

Vader disagreed. He knew of the *Millennium Falcon*'s power and was quite familiar with the skills of her cocky pilot. "No, Captain," he snarled angrily, "they're alive. I want every ship available to sweep the asteroid field until they're found."

As soon as Vader had given his command, Captain Needa's image and those of the other nineteen captains faded completely. When the last hologram vanished, the Dark Lord, having sensed the two men standing behind him, turned. "Now what is so important it couldn't wait, Admiral?" he asked imperiously. "Speak up!"

The admiral's face turned pale with fear, his trembling voice shaking almost as much as his body. "It was . . . the Emperor."

"The Emperor?" the voice behind the black breath mask repeated.

"Yes," the admiral replied. "He commands you make contact with him."

"Move this ship out of the asteroid field," Vader ordered, "into a position where we can send a clear transmission."

"Yes, my lord."

"And code the signal to my private chamber."

The *Millennium Falcon* had come to rest hidden in the small cave which was pitch black and dripping with moisture. The *Falcon*'s crew turned down its engines until no sound at all was emitted from the small craft.

Inside the cockpit, Han Solo and his shaggy copilot were just completing shutting down the ship's electronic systems. As they did so, all the service lights dimmed and the interior of the ship became nearly as dark as its sheltering cave.

Han glanced over at Leia and flashed her a quick grin. "Getting kind of romantic in here."

Chewbacca growled. There was work to be done in here and the Wookiee needed Han's undivided attention if they were going to repair the malfunctioning hyperdrive.

Irritated, Han returned to his work. "What are you so grouchy about?" he snapped.

Before the Wookiee could respond, the protocol droid timidly approached Han and posed a question of burning importance. "Sir, I'm almost afraid to ask, but does shutting down all except emergency power systems include me?"

Chewbacca expressed his opinion with a resounding bark of affirmation, but Han disagreed. "No," he said, "we're going to need you to talk to the old *Falcon* here and find out what happened to our hyperdrive." He looked over at the princess and added, "How are you with a macrofuser, Your Holiness?"

Before Leia could get off a suitable retort, the *Millennium Falcon* lurched forward as a sudden impact struck its hull. Everything that was not bolted down flew through the cockpit; even the giant Wookiee, howling boisterously, had to struggle to stay in his chair.

"Hang on!" Han yelled. "Watch out!"

See-Threepio clattered against a wall, then collected himself. "Sir, it's very possible this asteroid is not stable."

Han glared at him. "I'm glad you're here to tell us these things."

The ship rocked once more, even more violently than before.

The Wookiee howled again; Threepio stumbled backward, and Leia was hurled across the cabin directly into the waiting arms of Captain Solo.

The ship's rocking stopped as suddenly as it had started. But Leia still stood in Han's embrace. For once she did not draw away, and he could almost swear she was willingly embracing him. "Why, Princess," he said, pleasantly surprised, "this is so sudden."

At that, she began to pull back. "Let go," she insisted, trying to move out of his arms. "I'm getting angry."

Han saw the old familiar expression of arrogance beginning to return to her face. "You don't look angry," he lied.

"How do I look?"

"Beautiful," he answered truthfully, with an emotion that surprised him.

Leia felt suddenly, unexpectedly shy. Her cheeks flushed pink and, when she realized she was blushing, she averted her eyes. But she still did not really try to get free.

Han somehow couldn't let the tender moment last. "And excited," he had to add.

Leia became infuriated. Once again the angry princess and haughty senator, she quickly moved away from him and drew herself up to her most regal bearing. "Sorry, Captain," she said, her cheeks now reddened in anger, "being held by you isn't enough to get me excited."

"Well, I hope you don't expect more," he grunted, angrier at himself than at her stinging words.

"I don't expect anything," Leia said indignantly, "except to be left alone."

"If you'll just get out of my way, I'll leave you alone."

Embarrassed to realize that she was, indeed, still standing rather close, Leia stepped aside and made an effort to change the subject. "Don't you think it's time we got to work on your ship?"

Han frowned. "Fine with me," he said coldly, not looking at her.

Leia quickly turned on her heel and left the cockpit.

For a moment Han stood there quietly, just gathering his composure. Sheepishly he looked at the now quiet Wookiee and droid, both of whom had witnessed the entire incident.

"Come on, Chewie, let's tear into this flying short circuit," he said quickly to end the awkward moment.

The copilot barked in agreement, then joined his captain as they began to leave the cockpit. As they walked out, Han looked back at Threepio, who was still standing in the dim chamber looking dumbfounded. "You too, goldenrod!"

"I must admit," the robot muttered to himself as he began to shuffle out of the cockpit, "there are times I don't understand human behavior."

The lights of Luke Skywalker's X-wing fighter pierced the darkness of the bog planet. The ship had sunk deeper into the scummy waters, but there was still enough of it above the surface to let Luke carry needed supplies from the storage compartments. He knew it could not be much longer before his ship sank deeper—possibly all the way—beneath the water. He thought that his chance of survival might be increased if he gathered as many supplies as he could.

It was now so dark that Luke could scarcely see in front of him. Out in the dense jungle he heard a sharp snapping noise and felt a chill run through him. Grabbing his pistol, he prepared to blast anything that leaped from the jungle to attack him. But nothing did, and he clipped his weapon back onto its holster and continued to unpack his gear.

"You ready for some power?" Luke asked Artoo, who was patiently waiting for his own form of nourishment. Luke took a small fusion furnace from an equipment box and ignited it, welcoming even the tiny glow thrown off by the small heating device, then took a power cable and attached it to Artoo through a protuberance that roughly resembled a nose. As power radiated through Artoo's electronic innards, the stout robot whistled his appreciation.

Luke sat down and opened a container of processed food. As he began to eat, he talked to the robot. "Now all I have to do is find this Yoda, if he even exists."

He looked around nervously at the shadows in the jungle and felt frightened, miserable, and increasingly in doubt about his quest. "This certainly seems like a strange place to find a Jedi Master," he said to the little robot. "Gives me the creeps."

From the sound of his beep, it was clear Artoo shared Luke's opinion of the swamp world.

"Although," Luke continued as he reluctantly tasted more of the food, "there's something familiar about this place. I feel like—"

"You feel like what?"

That wasn't Artoo's voice! Luke leaped up, grabbed his pistol, then spun around, peering into the gloom to try to find the source of those words.

As he turned he saw a tiny creature standing directly in front of him. Luke immediately stepped back in surprise; this little being seemed to have materialized out of nowhere! It stood no more than half a meter in height, fearlessly holding its ground in front of the towering youth who wielded an awesome laser pistol.

The little wizened thing could have been any age. Its face was deeply lined, but was framed with elfin, pointed ears that gave it a look of eternal youth. Long white hair was parted down the middle and hung down on either side of the blue-skinned head. The being was bipedal, and stood on short legs that terminated in tridactyl, almost reptilian feet. It wore rags as gray as the mists of the swamp, and in such tatters that they must have approximated the creature's very age.

For the moment, Luke could not decide whether to be frightened or to laugh. But when he gazed into those bulbous eyes and sensed the being's kindly nature, he relaxed. At last the creature motioned toward the pistol in Luke's hand.

"Away put your weapon. I mean you no harm," it said.

After some hesitation, Luke quietly put his pistol back into his belt. As he did so, he wondered why he felt impelled to obey this little creature.

"I am wondering," the creature spoke again, "why are you here?"

"I'm looking for someone," Luke answered.

"Looking? Looking?" the creature repeated curiously with a wide smile beginning to crease his already-lined face. "You've found someone I'd say. Heh? Yes!"

Luke had to force himself not to smile. "Yeah."

"Help you I can . . . yes . . . yes."

Inexplicably Luke found himself trusting the odd creature, but wasn't at all sure that such a tiny individual could be of help on his important quest. "I don't think so," he replied gently. "You see, I'm looking for a great warrior."

"A *great* warrior?" The creature shook his head, the whitish hair flopping about his pointed ears. "Wars don't make one great."

A strange phrase, Luke thought. But before he could answer, Luke saw the tiny hominid hobble over to the top of the salvaged supply cases. Shocked, he watched as the creature began to rummage through the articles Luke had brought with him from Hoth.

"Get away from there," he said, surprised at this sudden strange behavior.

Moving across the ground, Artoo waddled toward the pile of cases, standing just about at optical sensor level with the creature. The droid squealed his disapproval as he scanned the creature that was carelessly digging through the supplies.

The strange being grabbed the container holding the remains of Luke's food and took a bite.

"Hey, that's my dinner!" Luke exclaimed.

But no sooner had the creature taken his first bite than he spat out what he had tasted, his deeply lined face wrinkling like a prune. *"Peewh!"* he said, spitting. "Thank you, no. How get you so big eating food of this kind?" He looked Luke up and down.

Before the astounded youth could reply, the creature flipped the food container in Luke's direction, then dipped one of his small and delicate hands into another supply case.

"Listen, friend," Luke said, watching this bizarre scavenger, "we didn't mean to land here. And if I could get my fighter out of this puddle I would, but I can't. So—"

"Can't get your ship out? Have you tried? Have you tried?" the creature goaded.

Luke had to admit to himself that he had not, but then the whole idea was patently ludicrous. He didn't have the proper equipment to—

Something in Luke's case had attracted the creature's interest. Luke finally reached the end of his patience when he saw the crazy little being snatch something out of the supply case. Knowing that survival depended on those supplies, he grabbed for the case. But the creature held on to his prize—a miniature power lamp that he gripped tightly in his blue-skinned hand. The little light came alive in the creature's hand, throwing its radiance up into his delighted face, and he immediately began to examine his treasure.

"Give me that!" Luke cried.

The creature retreated from the approaching youth like a petulant child. "Mine! Mine! Or I'll help you not."

Still clutching the lamp to his breast, the creature stepped backward, inadvertently bumping into Artoo-Detoo. Not remembering that the robot was at all animate, the being stood next to it as Luke approached.

"I don't want your help," Luke said indignantly. "I want my lamp back. I'll need it in this slimy mudhole."

Luke instantly realized he had issued an insult.

"Mudhole? Slimy? My home this is!"

As they argued, Artoo slowly reached out a mechanical arm. Suddenly his appendage grabbed the pilfered lamp and immediately the two little figures were engaged in a tug-of-war over the stolen prize. As they spun about in battle, Artoo beeped a few electronic, "give me that's."

"Mine, mine. Give it back," the creature cried. Abruptly, though, he seemed to give up the bizarre struggle and lightly poked the droid with one bluish finger.

Artoo emitted a loud, startled squeal and immediately released the power lamp.

The victor grinned at the glowing object in his tiny hands, gleefully repeating, "Mine, mine."

Luke was about fed up with these antics and advised the robot that the battle was over. "Okay, Artoo," he said with a sigh, "let him have it. Now get out of here, little fellow. We've got things to do."

"No, no!" the creature pleaded excitedly. "I'll stay and help you find your friend."

"I'm not looking for a friend," Luke said. "I'm looking for a Jedi Master."

"Oh, " the creature's eyes widened as he spoke, "a Jedi Master. Different altogether. *Yoda,* you seek, Yoda."

Mention of that name surprised Luke, but he felt skeptical. How could an elf like this know anything about a great teacher of the Jedi Knights? "You know him?"

"Of course, yes," the creature said proudly. "I'll take you to him. But first we must eat. Good food. Come, come."

With that, the creature scurried out of Luke's camp and into the shadows of the swamp. The tiny power lamp he carried was gradually dimming in the distance as Luke stood feeling baffled. At first he had no intention of pursuing the creature, but all at once he found himself diving into the fog after him.

As Luke started off into the jungle, he heard Artoo whistling and beeping as if he would blow his circuits. Luke turned around to see the little droid standing forlornly next to the miniature fission furnace.

"You'd better stay here and watch over the camp," Luke instructed the robot.

But Artoo only intensified his noisy output, running through the entire gamut of his electronic articulations.

"Artoo, now settle down," Luke called as he ran into the jungle. "I can take care of myself. I'll be safe, okay?"

Artoo's electronic grumblings grew fainter as Luke hurried to catch up with the little guide. I must really be out of my mind, Luke thought, following this weird being into who-knows-what. But the creature *had* mentioned Yoda's name, and Luke felt compelled to accept any help he could get to find the Jedi Master. He stumbled in the dark over thick weeds and twisting roots as he pursued the flickering light ahead.

The creature was chattering gaily as he led the way through the swamp. "Heh . . . safe . . . heh . . . quite safe . . . yes, of course." Then, in his odd little way, this mysterious being started to laugh.

Two Imperial cruisers slowly moved across the surface of the giant asteroid. The *Millennium Falcon* had to be hidden somewhere within—but where?

As the ships skimmed the surface of the asteroid, they dropped bombs on its pock-marked terrain, trying to scare out the freighter. The shock waves from the explosives violently shook the spheroid, but still there was no sign of the *Falcon*. As it drifted above the asteroid, one of the Imperial Star Destroyers cast an eclipsing shadow across the tunnel entrance. Yet the ship's scanners failed to note the curious hole in the bowllike wall. Within that hole, in a winding tunnel not detected by the minions of the powerful Empire, sat the freighter. It rattled and vibrated with every explosion that pounded the surface above.

Inside, Chewbacca worked feverishly to repair the complex powertrain. He had scrambled into an overhead compartment to get at the wires that operated the hyperdrive system. But when he felt the first of the explosions, he popped his head out through the mass of wires and gave out a worried yelp.

Princess Leia, who was welding a damaged valve, stopped her work and looked up. The bombs sounded very close.

See-Threepio glanced up at Leia and nervously tilted his head. "Oh, my," he said, "they've found us."

Everyone became quiet, as if fearing that the sound of their voices might somehow carry and betray their exact position. Again the ship was shaken by a blast, less intense than the last.

"They're moving away," Leia said.

Han saw through their tactic. "They're just trying to see if they can stir up something," he told her. "We're safe if we stay put."

"Where have I heard that line before?" Leia said with an innocent air.

Ignoring her sarcasm, Han moved past her as he went back to work. The passageway in the hold was so narrow that he couldn't avoid brushing against her as he passed by—or could he?

With mixed emotions the princess watched him

for a moment as he continued to work on his ship. And then she turned back to her welding.

See-Threepio ignored all this odd human behavior. He was too busy trying to communicate with the *Falcon,* trying to find out what was wrong with its hyperdrive. Standing at the central control panel, Threepio was making uncharacteristic whistle and beep sounds. A moment later, the control panel whistled back.

"Where is Artoo when I need him?" sighed the golden robot. The control panel's response had been difficult for him to interpret. "I don't know where your ship learned to communicate," Threepio announced to Han, "but its dialect leaves something to be desired. I believe, sir, it says the power coupling on the negative axis has been polarized. I'm afraid you'll have to replace it."

"Of course I'll have to replace it," Han snapped, then called up to Chewbacca, who was peering from the ceiling compartment. "Replace it!" he whispered.

He noticed that Leia had finished her welding but was having trouble reengaging the valve, struggling with a lever that simply would not budge. He moved toward her and began offering to help, but she coldly turned her back to him and continued her battle with the valve.

"Easy, Your Worship," he said. "Only trying to help."

Still struggling with the lever, Leia asked quietly, "Would you please stop calling me that?"

Han was surprised at the princess's simple tone. He had expected a stinging retort or, at best, a cold silence. But her words were missing the mocking tone that he was accustomed to hearing. Was she finally bringing their relentless battle of wills to an end? "Sure," he said gently.

"You make things difficult sometimes," Leia said as she shyly glanced at him.

He had to agree. "I do, I really do." But he added, "You could be a little nicer, too. Come on, admit it, sometimes you think I'm all right."

She let go of the lever and rubbed her sore hand. "Sometimes," she said with a little smile, "maybe . . . occasionally, when you aren't acting the scoundrel."

"Scoundrel?" he laughed, finding her choice of words endearing. "I like the sound of that."

Without another word, he reached for Leia's hand and began to massage it.

"Stop it," Leia protested.

Han continued to hold her hand. "Stop what?" he asked softly.

Leia felt flustered, confused, embarrassed—a hundred things in that moment. But her sense of dignity prevailed. "Stop that!" she said regally. "My hands are dirty."

Han smiled at her feeble excuse, but held on to her hand and looked right into her eyes. "My hands are dirty, too. What are you afraid of?"

"Afraid?" She returned his direct gaze. "Of getting my hands dirty."

"That's why you're trembling?" he asked. He could see that she was affected by his closeness and by his touch, and her expression softened. Whereupon he reached out and took her other hand.

"I think you like me *because* I'm a scoundrel," he said. "I think you haven't had *enough* scoundrels in your life." As he spoke he slowly drew her near.

Leia didn't resist his gentle pull. Now, as she

looked at him, she thought he had never seemed more handsome, but she was still the princess. "I happen to *like* nice men," she chided in a whisper.

"And I'm not nice?" Han asked, teasing.

Chewbacca stuck his head out from the overhead compartment and watched the proceedings unnoticed.

"Yes," she whispered, "but you . . ."

Before she could finish, Han Solo drew her to him and felt her body tremble as he pressed his lips to hers. It seemed forever, it seemed an eternity to share between them, as he gently bent her body back. This time she didn't resist at all.

When they parted, Leia needed a moment to catch her breath. She tried to regain her composure and work up a measure of indignation, but she found it difficult to talk.

"Okay, hot shot," she began. "I—"

But then she stopped, and suddenly found herself kissing him, pulling him even closer than before.

When their lips finally parted, Han held Leia in his arms as they looked at each other. For a long moment there was a peaceful kind of emotion between them. Then Leia began to draw away, her thoughts and feelings a turmoil. She averted her eyes and began to disengage herself from Han's embrace. In the next second she turned and rushed from the cabin.

Han silently looked after her as she left the room. He then became acutely aware of the very curious Wookiee whose head was poking from the ceiling.

"Okay, Chewie!" he bellowed. "Give me a hand with this valve."

The fog, dispersed by a torrent of rain, snaked around the swamp in diaphanous swirls. Scooting along amid the pounding rain was a single R2 droid looking for his master.

Artoo-Detoo's sensing devices were busily sending impulses to his electronic nerve ends. At the slightest sound, his auditory systems reacted—perhaps overreacted—and sent information to the robot's nervous computer brain.

It was too wet for Artoo in this murky jungle. He aimed his optical sensors in the direction of a strange little mud house on the edge of a dark lake. The robot, overtaken by an almost-human perception of loneliness, moved closer to the window of the tiny abode. Artoo extended his utility feet toward the window and peeked inside. He hoped no one inside noticed the slight shiver of his barrel-shaped form or heard his nervous little electronic whimper.

Somehow Luke Skywalker managed to squeeze inside the miniature house, where everything within was perfectly scaled to its tiny resident. Luke sat cross-legged on the dried mud floor in the living room, careful not to bang his skull against the low ceiling. There was a table in front of him and he could see a few containers holding what appeared to be hand-written scrolls.

The wrinkle-faced creature was in his kitchen, next to the living room, busily concocting an incredible meal. From where Luke sat he could see the little cook stirring steaming pots, chopping this, shredding that, scattering herbs over all, and scurrying back and forth to put platters on the table in front of the youth.

Fascinated as he was by this bustling activity, Luke was growing very impatient. As the creature made one of his frantic runs into the living room area, Luke reminded his host, "I told you, I'm not hungry."

"Patience," the creature said, as he scuttled back into the steamy kitchen. "It's time to eat."

Luke tried to be polite. "Look,'" he said, "it smells good. I'm sure it's delicious. But I don't know why we can't see Yoda now."

"It's the Jedi's time to eat, too," the creature answered.

But Luke was eager to be on his way. "Will it take long to get there? How far is he?"

"Not far, not far. Be patient. Soon you will see him. Why wish you become a Jedi?"

"Because of my father, I guess," Luke answered, as he reflected that he never really knew his father that well. In truth his deepest kinship with his father was through the lightsaber Ben had entrusted to him.

Luke noticed the curious look in the creature's eyes as he mentioned his father. "Oh, your father," the being said, sitting down to begin his vast meal. "A powerful Jedi was he. Powerful Jedi."

The youth wondered if the creature were mocking him. "How could you know my father?" he asked a little angrily. "You don't even know who I am." He glanced around at the bizarre room and shook his head. "I don't know what I'm doing here . . ."

Then he noticed that the creature had turned away from him and was talking to a corner of the room. This really is the final straw, Luke thought. Now this impossible creature is talking to thin air!

"No good is this," the creature was saying irritably. "This will not do. I cannot teach him. The boy has no patience!"

Luke's head spun in the direction the creature was facing. *Cannot teach. No patience.* Bewildered, he still saw no one there. Then the truth of the situation gradually became as plain to him as the deep lines on the little creature's face. Already he was being tested—and by none other than Yoda himself!

From the empty corner of the room, Luke heard the gentle, wise voice of Ben Kenobi responding to Yoda. "He will learn patience," Ben said.

"Much anger in him," the dwarfish Jedi teacher persisted. "Like in his father."

"We've discussed this before," Kenobi said.

Luke could no longer wait. "I *can* be a Jedi," he interrupted. It meant more than anything else to him to become a part of the noble band that had championed the causes of justice and peace. "I'm ready, Ben . . . Ben . . ." The youth called to his invisible mentor, looking about the room in hopes of finding him. But all he saw was Yoda sitting across from him at the table.

"Ready are you?" the skeptical Yoda asked. "What know you of ready? I have trained Jedi for eight hundred years. My own counsel I'll keep on who is to be trained."

"Why not me?" Luke asked, insulted by Yoda's insinuation.

"To become a Jedi," Yoda said gravely, "takes the deepest commitment, the most serious mind."

"He can do it," Ben's voice said in defense of the youth.

Looking toward the invisible Kenobi, Yoda pointed at Luke. "This one I have watched a long time. All his life has he looked away . . . to the horizon, to the sky, to the future. Never his mind on where he was, on what he was doing. Adventure, excitement." Yoda shot a glaring look at Luke. "A Jedi craves not these things!"

Luke tried to defend his past. "I have followed my feelings."

"You are reckless!" the Jedi Master shouted.

"He will learn," came the soothing voice of Kenobi.

"He's too old," Yoda argued. "Yes. Too old, too set in his ways to start the training."

Luke thought he heard a subtle softening in Yoda's voice. Perhaps there was still a chance to sway him. "I've learned much," Luke said. He couldn't give up now. He had come too far, endured too much, *lost* too much for that.

Yoda seemed to look right through Luke as he spoke those words, as if trying to determine how much he *had* learned. He turned to the invisible Kenobi again. "Will he finish what he begins?" Yoda asked.

"We've come this far," was the answer. "He is our only hope."

"I will not fail you," Luke said to both Yoda and Ben. "I'm not afraid." And, indeed, at that moment, the young Skywalker felt he could face anything without fear.

But Yoda was not so optimistic. "You will be, my young one," he warned. The Jedi Master turned slowly to face Luke as a strange little smile appeared on his blue face. "Heh. You will be."'

☐ IX

ONLY one being in the entire universe could instill fear in the dark spirit of Darth Vader. As he stood, silent and alone in his dim chamber, the Dark Lord of the Sith waited for a visit from his own dreaded master.

As he waited, his Imperial Star Destroyer floated through a vast ocean of stars. No one on his ship would have dared disturb Darth Vader in his private cubicle. But if they had, they might have detected a slight trembling in that black-cloaked frame. And there might even have been a hint of terror to be seen upon his visage, had anyone been able to see through his concealing black breath mask.

But no one approached, and Vader remained motionless as he kept his lonely, patient vigil. Soon a strange electronic whine broke the dead silence of the room and a flickering light began to glimmer on the Dark Lord's cloak. Vader immediately bowed deeply in homage to his royal master.

The visitor arrived in the form of a hologram that materialized before Vader and towered above him. The three-dimensional figure was clad in simple robes and its face was concealed behind an enormous hood.

When the hologram of the Galactic Emperor finally spoke, it did so with a voice even deeper than Vader's. The Emperor's presence was awesome enough, but the sound of his voice sent a thrill of terror coursing through Vader's powerful frame. "You may rise, my servant," the Emperor commanded.

Immediately Vader straightened up. But he did not dare gaze into his master's face, and instead cast his eyes down at his own black boots.

"What is thy bidding, my master?" Vader asked with all the solemnity of a priest attending his god.

"There is a grave disturbance in the Force," the Emperor said.

"I have felt it," the Dark Lord replied solemnly.

The Emperor emphasized the danger as he continued. "Our situation is most precarious. We have a new enemy who could bring about our destruction."

"Our destruction? Who?"

"The son of Skywalker. You must destroy him, or he will be our undoing."

Skywalker!

The thought was impossible. How could the Emperor be concerned with this insignificant youth?

"He's not a Jedi," Vader reasoned. "He's just a boy. Obi-Wan could not have taught him so much that—"

The Emperor broke in. "The Force is strong in him," he insisted. "He must be destroyed."

The Dark Lord reflected for a moment. Perhaps there was another way to deal with the boy, a way that might benefit the Imperial cause. "If he could be turned, he would be a powerful ally," Vader suggested.

Silently the Emperor considered the possibility.

After a moment, he spoke again. "Yes . . . yes," he said thoughtfully. "He would be a great asset. Can it be done?"

For the first time in their meeting, Vader lifted his head to face his master directly. "He will join us," he answered firmly, "or die, my master."

With that, the encounter had come to an end. Vader kneeled before the Galactic Emperor, who passed his hand over his obedient servant. In the next moment, the holographic image had completely disappeared, leaving Darth Vader alone to formulate what would be, perhaps, his most subtle plan of attack.

The indicator lights on the control panel cast an eerie glow through the quiet cockpit of the *Millennium Falcon*. They softly lit Princess Leia's face as she sat in the pilot's chair, thinking about Han. Deep in thought, she ran her hand along the control panel in front of her. She knew something was churned up within her, but wasn't certain that she was willing to acknowledge it. And yet, could she deny it?

Suddenly her attention was attracted by a flurry of movement outside the cockpit window. A dark shape, at first too swift and too shadowy to identify, streaked toward the *Millennium Falcon*. In an instant it had attached itself to the ship's front window with something that looked like a soft suction cup. Cautiously Leia moved forward for a closer look at the black smudgelike shape. As she peered out the window, a set of large yellow eyes suddenly popped open and stared right at her.

Leia started in shock and stumbled backward into the pilot's seat. As she tried to compose herself, she heard the scurry of feet and an inhuman screech. Suddenly the black shape and its yellow eyes disappeared into the darkness of the asteroid cave.

She caught her breath, leaped up out of the chair, and raced to the ship's hold.

The *Falcon*'s crew was finishing its work on the ship's power system. As they worked, the lights flickered weakly, then came on and stayed on brightly. Han finished reconnecting the wires, and began setting a floor panel back in place while the Wookiee watched See-Threepio complete his work at the control panel.

"Everything checks out here," Threepio reported. "If I might say so, I believe that should do it."

Just then, the princess rushed breathlessly into the hold.

"There's something out there!" Leia cried.

Han looked up from his work. "Where?"

"Outside," she said, "in the cave."

As she spoke, they heard a sharp banging against the ship's hull. Chewbacca looked up and let out a loud bark of concern.

"Whatever it is sounds like it's trying to get in," Threepio observed worriedly.

The captain began to move out of the hold. "I'm going to see what it is," he announced.

"Are you crazy?" Leia looked at him in astonishment.

The banging was getting louder.

"Look, we just got this bucket going again," Han explained. "I'm not about to let some varmint tear it apart."

Before Leia could protest, he had grabbed a breath mask off a supply rack and pulled it down over his head. As Han walked out, the Wookiee hurried up behind him and grabbed his own face mask Leia realized that, as part of the crew, she was duty-bound to join them.

"If there's more than one," she told the captain, "you're going to need help."

Han looked at her affectionately as she removed a third breath mask and placed it over her lovely, but determined. face.

Then the three of them rushed out, leaving the protocol droid to complain pitifully to the empty hold: "But that leaves me here all alone!"

The darkness outside the *Millennium Falcon* was thick and dank. It surrounded the three figures as they carefully moved around their ship. With each step they heard unsettling noises, *squishing* sounds, that echoed through the dripping cavern.

It was too dark to tell where the creature might be hiding. They moved cautiously, peering as well as they could into the deep gloom. Suddenly Chewbacca, who could see better in the dark than either his captain or the princess, emitted a muffled bark and pointed toward the thing that moved along the *Falcon*'s hull.

A shapeless leathery mass scurried over the top of the ship, apparently startled by the Wookiee's yelp Han leveled his blaster at the creature and blasted the thing with a laser bolt. The black shape screeched, stumbled, then fell off the spaceship, landing with a *thud* at the princess's feet.

She leaned over to get a better look at the black mass. "Looks like some kind of Mynock," she told Han and Chewbacca

Han glanced quickly around the dark tunnel. "There will be more of them," he predicted. "They always travel in groups. And there's nothing they like better than to attach themselves to ships. Just what we need right now!"

But Leia was more distracted by the consistency of the tunnel floor. The tunnel itself struck her as peculiar; the smell of the place was unlike that of any cave she had ever known. The floor was especially cold and seemed to cling to her feet.

As she stamped her foot against the floor, she felt the ground give a bit beneath her heel. "This asteroid has the strangest consistency," she said. "Look at the ground. It's not like rock at all."

Han knelt to inspect the floor more closely and noted how pliable it was. As he studied the floor, he tried to make out how far it reached and to see the contours of the cave.

"There's an awful lot of moisture in here," he said. He stood up and aimed his hand blaster at the far side of the cave, then fired toward the sound of a screeching Mynock in the distance; as soon as he shot the bolt, the entire cavern began to shake and the ground began to buckle. "I was afraid of that," he shouted. "Let's get out of here!"

Chewbacca barked in agreement, and bolted toward the *Millennium Falcon*. Close behind him, Leia and Han rushed toward the ship, covering their faces as a swarm of Mynocks flew past them. They reached the *Falcon* and ran up the platform into the ship. As soon as they were on board, Chewbacca closed the hatch after them, careful that none of the Mynocks could slip inside.

"Chewie, fire her up!" Han yelled as he and Leia darted through the ship's hold. "We're getting out of here!"

Chewbacca hurriedly lumbered to his seat in the cockpit, while Han rushed to check the scopes on the hold control panel.

Leia, running to keep up, warned, "They would spot us long before we could get up to speed."

Han didn't seem to hear her. He checked the controls, then turned to rush back to the cockpit. But as he passed her, his comment made it clear he had heard every word. "There's no time to discuss this in committee."

And with that he was gone, racing to his pilot's chair, where he began working the engine throttles. The next minute the whine of the main engines resounded through the ship.

But Leia hurried after him. "I am not a committee," she shouted indignantly.

It didn't appear that he heard her. The sudden cave-quake was beginning to subside, but Han was determined to get his ship out—and out fast.

Leia began to strap herself into her seat.

"You can't make the jump to light-speed in this asteroid field," she called over the engine roar.

Solo grinned at her over his shoulder. "Strap yourself in, sweetheart," he said, "we're taking off!"

"But the tremors have stopped!"

Han was not about to stop his ship now. Already the craft moved forward, quickly passing the craggy walls of the tunnel. Suddenly Chewbacca barked in horror as he stared out the front windscreen.

Directly in front of them stood a jagged white row of stalactites and stalagmites completely surrounding the cave's entrance.

"I see it, Chewie," Han shouted. He pulled hard on the throttle, and the *Millennium Falcon* surged forward. "Hang on!"

"The cave is collapsing," Leia screamed as she saw the entrance ahead grow smaller.

"This is no cave."

"What?!"

Threepio began jabbering in terror. "Oh, my, no! We're doomed. Good-bye, Mistress Leia. Good-bye, Captain."

Leia's mouth dropped open as she stared at the rapidly approaching tunnel opening.

Han was right; they were not in a cave. As they came nearer the opening, it was apparent that the white mineral formations were giant teeth. And it was very apparent that, as they soared out of this giant mouth, those teeth were beginning to close!

Chewbacca roared.

"Bank, Chewie!"

It was an impossible maneuver. But Chewbacca responded immediately and once again accomplished the impossible. He rolled the *Millennium Falcon* steeply on its side, tilting the ship as he accelerated it between two of those gleaming white fangs. And not a second too soon, for just as the *Falcon* flew from that living tunnel, the jaws clamped shut.

The *Falcon* sped through the rocky crevice of the asteroid, pursued by a titanic space slug. The enormous pink bulk didn't intend to lose its tasty meal and pushed itself out of its crater to swallow the escaping ship. But the monster was too slow. Within another moment the freighter had soared out, away from the slimy pursuer and into space. As it did so, the ship plunged into yet another danger: The *Millennium Falcon* had re-entered the deadly asteroid field.

Luke was panting, nearly out of breath in this, the latest of his endurance tests. His Jedi taskmaster had ordered him out on a marathon run through the dense growth of his planet's jungle. Not only had Yoda sent Luke on the exhausting run, but he had invited himself along for the ride. As the Jedi-in-training puffed and sweated his way on his rugged race, the little Jedi Master observed his progress from a pouch strapped to Luke's back.

Yoda shook his head and muttered to himself disparagingly about the youth's lack of endurance.

By the time they returned to the clearing where Artoo-Detoo was patiently waiting, Luke's exhaustion had nearly overcome him. As he stumbled into the clearing, Yoda had yet another test planned for him.

Before Luke had caught his breath, the little Jedi on his back tossed a metal bar in front of Luke's eyes. In an instant Luke ignited his laser sword and swung frantically at the bar. But he was not fast enough, and the bar fell—untouched—onto the ground with a thud. Luke collapsed on the wet earth in complete exhaustion. "I can't," he moaned, ". . . too tired."

Yoda, who showed no sign of sympathy, retorted, "It would be in seven pieces, were you a Jedi."

But Luke knew that he was not a Jedi—not yet, anyway. And the rigorous training program devised by Yoda had left him nearly out of breath. "I thought I was in good shape," he gasped.

"Yes, but by what standard, ask I?" the little instructor quizzed. "Forget your old measures. Unlearn, unlearn!"

Luke truly felt ready to unlearn all his old ways and willing to free himself to learn all this Jedi Master had to teach. It was rigorous training, but as time passed, Luke's strength and abilities increased and even his skeptical little master began to see hope. But it was not easy.

Yoda spent long hours lecturing his student about

the ways of the Jedi. As they sat under the trees near Yoda's little house, Luke listened intently to all the master's tales and lessons. And as Luke listened, Yoda chewed on his Gimer Stick, a short twig with three small branches at the far end.

And there were physical tests of all kinds. In particular, Luke was working hard to perfect his leap. Once he felt ready to show Yoda his improvement. As the master sat on a log next to a wide pond, he heard the loud rustling of someone approaching through the vegetation.

Suddenly Luke appeared on the other side of the pond, coming toward the water at a run. As he approached the shore, he made a running leap toward Yoda, rising high above the water as he hurtled himself through the air. But he fell short of the other side and landed in the water with a loud splash, completely soaking Yoda.

Yoda's blue lips turned down in disappointment.

But Luke was not about to give up. He was determined to become a Jedi and, no matter how foolish he might feel in the attempt, would pass every test Yoda set for him. So he didn't complain when Yoda told him to stand on his head. A bit awkwardly at first, Luke inverted his body and, after a few wobbly moments, was standing firmly on his hands. It seemed he had been in this position for hours, but it was less difficult than it would have been before his training. His concentration had improved so much that he was able to maintain a perfect balance—even with Yoda perched on the soles of his feet.

But that was only part of the test. Yoda signaled Luke by tapping on his leg with his Gimer Stick. Slowly, carefully, and with full concentration, Luke raised one hand off the ground. His body wavered slightly with the weight shift—but Luke kept his balance, and, concentrating, started to lift a small rock in front of him. But suddenly a whistling and beeping R2 unit came rushing up to his youthful master.

Luke collapsed, and Yoda jumped clear of his falling body. Annoyed, the young Jedi student asked, "Oh, Artoo, what is it?"

Artoo-Detoo rolled about in frantic circles as he tried to communicate his message through a series of electronic chirps. Luke watched as the droid scooted to the edge of the swamp. He hurried to follow and then saw what it was the little robot was trying to tell him.

Standing at the water's edge, Luke saw that all but the tip of the X-wing's nose had disappeared beneath the water's surface.

"Oh, no," moaned Luke. "We'll never get it out now."

Yoda had joined them, and stamped his foot in irritation at Luke's remark. "So sure are you?" Yoda scolded. "Tried have you? Always with you it can't be done. Hear you nothing that I say?" His little wrinkled face puckered with a furious scowl.

Luke glanced at his master, then looked doubtfully toward the sunken ship.

"Master," he said skeptically, "lifting rocks is one thing, but this is a little different." Yoda was really angry now. "No! No different!" he shouted. "The differences are in your mind. Throw them out! No longer of use are they to you."

Luke trusted his master. If Yoda said this could be done, then maybe he should try. He looked at the downed X-wing and readied himself for maximum concentration. "Okay," he said at last, "I'll give it a try."

Again he had spoken the wrong words. "No," Yoda said impatiently. "Try not. *Do, do.* Or do not. There is no try."

Luke closed his eyes. He tried to envision the contours, the shape, to feel the weight of his X-wing fighter. And he concentrated on the movement it would make as it rose from the murky waters.

As he concentrated, he began to hear the waters churn and gurgle, and then begin to bubble with the emerging nose of the X-wing. The tip of the fighter was slowly lifting from the water, and it hovered there for a moment, then sank back beneath the surface with a loud splash.

Luke was drained and had to gasp for breath. "I can't," he said dejectedly. "It's too big."

"Size has no meaning," Yoda insisted. "It matters not. Look at *me*. Judge me by my *size,* do you?"

Luke, chastened, just shook his head.

"And well you shouldn't," the Jedi Master advised. "For my ally is the Force. And a powerful ally it is. Life creates it and makes it grow. Its energy surrounds us and binds us. Luminous beings we are, not this crude matter," he said as he pinched Luke's skin.

Yoda made a grand sweeping gesture to indicate the vastness of the universe about him. "Feel it you must. Feel the flow. Feel the Force around you. Here," he said, as he pointed, "between you and me and that tree and that rock."

While Yoda gave his explanation of the Force, Artoo spun his domed head around, trying without success to register this "Force" on his scanners. He whistled and beeped in bafflement.

"Yes, everywhere," Yoda continued, ignoring the little droid, "waiting to be felt and used. Yes, even between this land and that ship!"

Then Yoda turned and looked at the swamp, and as he did the water began to swirl. Slowly, from the gently bubbling waters, the nose of the fighter appeared again.

Luke gaped in astonishment as the X-wing gracefully rose from its watery tomb and moved majestically toward the shore.

He silently vowed never to use the word "impossible" again. For there, standing on his tree root pedestal, was tiny Yoda, effortlessly gliding the ship from the water onto the shore. It was a sight that Luke could scarcely believe. But he knew that it was a potent example of Jedi mastery over the Force.

Artoo, equally astounded but not so philosophical, issued a series of loud whistles, then bolted off to hide behind some giant roots.

The X-wing seemed to float onto the beach, and then gently came to a stop.

Luke was humbled by the feat he had witnessed and approached Yoda in awe. "I . . ." he began, dazzled. "I don't believe it."

"That," Yoda stated emphatically, "is why you fail."

Bewildered, Luke shook his head, wondering if he would ever rise to the station of a Jedi.

Bounty hunters! Among the most reviled of the galaxy's inhabitants, this class of amoral money-grubbers included members of every species. It was a repellent occupation, and it often attracted repellent creatures to its fold. Some of these creatures had been summoned by Darth Vader and now stood with him on the bridge of his Imperial Star Destroyer.

Admiral Piett observed this motley group from a distance as he stood with one of Vader's captains. They saw that the Dark Lord had invited a particularly bizarre assortment of fortune hunters, including Bossk, whose soft, baggy face gawked at Vader with huge bloodshot orbs. Next to Bossk stood Zuckuss and Dengar, two human types, battle-scarred by innumerable, unspeakable adventures. A battered and tarnished chrome-colored droid named IG-88 was also with the group, standing next to the notorious Boba Fett. A human bounty hunter, Fett was known for his extremely ruthless methods. He was dressed in a weapon-covered, armored spacesuit, the kind worn by a group of evil warriors defeated by the Jedi Knights during the Clone Wars. A few braided scalps completed his unsavory image. The very sight of Boba Fett sent a shudder of revulsion through the admiral.

"Bounty hunters!" Piett said with disdain. "Why should he bring them into this? The Rebels won't escape us."

Before the captain could reply, a ship's controller rushed up to the admiral. "Sir," he said urgently, "we have a priority signal from the Star Destroyer *Avenger*."

Admiral Piett read the signal, then hurried to inform Darth Vader. As he approached the group, Piett heard the last of Vader's instructions to them. "There will be a substantial reward for the one who finds the *Millennium Falcon*," he was saying. "You are free to use any methods necessary, but I want proof. No disintegrations."

The Sith Lord stopped his briefing as Admiral Piett hurried to his side.

"My lord," the admiral whispered ecstatically, "we have them!"

X

THE *Avenger* had spotted the *Millennium Falcon* the moment the freighter shot out of the enormous asteroid.

From that moment, the Imperial ship renewed its pursuit of the freighter with a blinding barrage of fire. Undaunted by the steady rain of asteroids on its massive hull, the Star Destroyer relentlessly followed the smaller ship.

The *Millennium Falcon,* far more maneuverable than the other ship, darted around the larger asteroids as they came rocketing toward it. The *Falcon* was succeeding in holding its lead in front of the *Avenger,* but it was clear that the steadily pursuing ship was not about to abandon the chase.

Suddenly a gigantic asteroid appeared in the *Millennium Falcon*'s path, rushing toward the freighter at incredible speed. The ship quickly banked out of the way, and the asteroid hurtled past it, only to explode harmlessly against the *Avenger*'s hull.

Han Solo glimpsed the explosion's flare through the front window of his ship's cockpit. The craft that followed them seemed absolutely invulnerable; but he had no time to reflect on the differences between the ships. It took everything in his power to maintain control of the *Falcon* as it was pelted by Imperial cannon fire.

Princess Leia tensely watched the asteroids and cannon fire flaring in the blackness of space outside the cockpit windows. Her fingers had tightened on the arms of her chair. Silently she hoped against hope that they would emerge from this chase alive.

Carefully following the bleeping images on a tracking scope, See-Threepio turned to Han. "I can see the edge of the asteroid field, sir," he reported.

"Good," Han replied. "Soon as we're clear, we'll kick this baby into hyperdrive." He was confident that within moments the pursuing Star Destroyer would be left light-years behind. The repairs in the freighter's light-speed systems had been completed, and there was nothing left to do now but get the ship free of the asteroid field and into space, where it could blast away to safety.

There was an excited Wookiee bark as Chewbacca, looking out a cockpit window, saw that the asteroid density was already decreasing. But their escape could not yet be completed, for the *Avenger* was closing in, and the bolts from its laser cannons bombarded the *Falcon,* making it lurch and carom to one side.

Han rapidly adjusted the controls and brought his ship back on an even keel. And in the next instant, the *Falcon* zoomed out of the asteroid field and entered the peaceful, star-dotted silence of deep space. Chewbacca whined, joyful that they were at last out of the deadly field—but eager to leave the Star Destroyer far behind.

"I'm with you, Chewie," Han responded. "Let's vacate the area. Stand by for light-speed. This time *they* get the surprise. Hang on . . ."

Everyone braced himself as Han pulled back on the light-speed throttle. But it was the crew of the

Millennium Falcon, and mostly the captain himself, that got the surprise as, once again—

—nothing happened.

Nothing!

Han frantically pulled back the throttle again. The ship maintained its sublight speed.

"This isn't fair!" he exclaimed, beginning to panic.

Chewbacca was furious. It was rare that he lost his temper with his friend and captain. But now he was exasperated and roared his fury in angry Wookiee growls and barks.

"Couldn't be," Han replied defensively, as he looked at his computer screens and quickly noted their readings. "I checked the transfer circuits."

Chewbacca barked again.

"I tell you, this time it's not my fault. I'm *sure* I checked it."

Leia sighed deeply. "No light-speed?" in a tone that indicated she had expected *this* catastrophe, too.

"Sir," See-Threepio interjected, "we've lost the rear deflector shield. One more direct hit on the back quarter and we're done for."

"Well," Leia said, as she glared at the captain of the *Millennium Falcon,* "what now?"

Han realized he had only one choice. There was no time to plan or to check computer readouts, not with the *Avenger* already out of the asteroid field and rapidly gaining on them. He had to make a decision based on instinct and hope. They really had no alternative.

"Sharp bank, Chewie," he ordered and pulled back a lever as he looked at his copilot. "Let's turn this bucket around."

Not even Chewbacca could fathom what Han

had in mind. He barked in bewilderment—perhaps he hadn't heard the order quite right.

"You heard me!" Han yelled. "Turn around! Full power front shield!" This time there was no mistaking his command and, though Chewbacca couldn't comprehend the suicidal maneuver, he obeyed.

The princess was flabbergasted. "You're going to attack them!" she stammered in disbelief. There wasn't a *chance* of survival now, she thought. Was it possible that Han really was crazy?

Threepio, after running some calculations through his computer brain, turned to Han Solo. "Sir, if I might point out, the odds of surviving a direct assault on an Imperial Star Destroyer are—"

Chewbacca snarled at the golden droid, and Threepio immediately shut up. No one on board really wanted to hear the statistics, especially since the *Falcon* was already banking into a steep turn to begin its course into the erupting storm of Imperial cannon fire.

Solo concentrated intently on his flying. It was all he could do to avoid the barrage of flak bursts rocketing toward the *Falcon* from the Imperial ship. The freighter bobbed and weaved as Han, still heading directly for the Star Destroyer, steered to avoid the bolts.

No one on his tiny ship had the slightest idea what his plan might be.

"He's coming in too low!" the Imperial deck officer shouted, though he scarcely believed what he was seeing.

Captain Needa and the Star Destroyer crew rushed to the *Avenger*'s bridge to watch the suicidal approach of the *Millennium Falcon,* while alarms blared all over the vast Imperial ship. A small freighter could not do much damage if it collided against a Star Destroyer's hull; but if it smashed through the bridge windows, the control deck would be littered with corpses.

The panicked tracking officer reported his sighting. "We're going to collide!"

"Shields up?" Captain Needa asked. "He must be insane!"

"Look out!" the deck officer yelled.

The *Falcon* was headed straight for the bridge window and the *Avenger* crew and officers fell to the floor in terror. But at the last instant, the freighter veered up sharply. Then—

Captain Needa and his men slowly lifted their heads. All they saw outside the bridge windows was a peaceful ocean of stars.

"Track them," Captain Needa ordered. "They may come around for another pass."

The tracking officer attempted to find the freighter on his scopes. But there was nothing to find.

"That's strange," he muttered.

"What is it?" Needa asked, walking over to look at the tracking monitors for himself.

"The ship doesn't appear on any of our scopes."

The captain was perplexed. "It couldn't have disappeared. Could a ship that small have a cloaking device?"

"No, sir," the deck officer answered. "Maybe they went into light-speed at the last minute."

Captain Needa felt his anger mounting at about the same rate as his befuddlement. "Then why did they attack? They could have gone into hyperspace when they cleared the asteroid field."

"Well, there's no trace of them, sir, no matter

how they did it," the tracking officer replied, still unable to locate the *Millennium Falcon* on his viewers. "The only logical explanation is that they went into light-speed."

The captain was staggered. How had that crate of a ship eluded him?

An aide approached. "Sir, Lord Vader demands an update on the pursuit," he reported. "What should he be told?"

Needa braced himself. Letting the *Millennium Falcon* get away when it was so close was an unforgiveable error, and he knew he had to face Vader and report his failure. He felt resigned to whatever punishment waited in store for him.

"I am responsible for this," he said. "Get the shuttle ready. When we rendezvous with Lord Vader, I will apologize to him myself. Turn around and scan the area one more time."

Then, like a living behemoth, the great *Avenger* slowly began to turn; but there was still no sign of the *Millennium Falcon*.

The two glowing balls hovered like alien fireflies above Luke's body lying motionless in the mud. Standing protectively next to his fallen master, a little barrel-shaped droid periodically extended a mechanical appendage to swat at the dancing objects as if they were mosquitoes. But the hovering balls of light leaped just out of the robot's reach.

Artoo-Detoo leaned over Luke's inert body and whistled in an effort to revive him. But Luke, stunned unconscious by the charges of these energy balls, did not respond. The robot turned to Yoda, who was sitting calmly on a tree stump, and angrily began to beep and scold the little Jedi Master.

Getting no sympathy from him, Artoo turned back to Luke. His electronic circuits told him there was no use trying to wake Luke with his little noises. An emergency rescue system was activated within his metal hull and Artoo extended a small metal electrode and rested it on Luke's chest. Uttering a quiet beep of concern, Artoo generated a mild electrical charge, just strong enough to jolt Luke back to consciousness. The youth's chest heaved, and he awoke with a start.

Looking dazed, the young Jedi student shook his head clear. He looked around him, rubbing his shoulders to ease the ache from Yoda's seeker balls' attack. Glimpsing the seekers still suspended over him, Luke scowled. Then he heard Yoda chuckling merrily nearby, and turned his glare on him.

"Concentration, heh?" Yoda laughed, his lined face creased with enjoyment. "Concentration!"

Luke was in no mood to return his smile. "I thought those seekers were set for stun!" he exclaimed angrily.

"That they are," the amused Yoda answered.

"They're a lot stronger than I'm used to." Luke's shoulder ached painfully.

"That would not matter were the Force flowing through you," Yoda reasoned. "Higher you'd jump! Faster you'd move!" he exclaimed. "Open yourself to the Force you must."

The youth was beginning to feel exasperated with his arduous training, although he had only been at it a short time. He had felt very close to knowing the Force—but so many times he had failed and had realized how very far away it was from him still. But now Yoda's goading words made him spring to his feet. He was tired of waiting so long for this power, weary at his lack of success, and increasingly infuriated by Yoda's cryptic teachings.

Luke grabbed his laser sword from the mud and quickly ignited it.

Terrified, Artoo-Detoo scurried away to safety.

"I'm open to it now!" Luke shouted. "I feel it. Come on, you little flying blasters!" With fire in his eyes, Luke poised his weapon and moved toward the seekers. Immediately they zipped away and retreated to hover over Yoda.

"No, no," the Jedi Master scolded, shaking his hoary head. "This will not do. *Anger* is what you feel."

"But I feel the Force!" Luke protested vehemently.

"Anger, anger, fear, aggression!" Yoda warned. "The dark side of the Force are they. Easily *they* flow . . . quick to join in a fight. Beware, beware, beware of them. A heavy price is paid for the power they bring."

Luke lowered his sword and stared at Yoda in confusion. "Price?" he asked. "What do you mean?"

"The dark side beckons," Yoda said dramatically. "But if once start you down the dark path, forever will it dominate your destiny. Consume you it will . . . as it did Obi-Wan's apprentice."

Luke nodded. He knew who Yoda meant. "Lord Vader," he said. After he thought for a moment, Luke asked, "Is the dark side stronger?"

"No, no. Easier, quicker, more seductive."

"But how am I to know the good side from the bad?" he asked, puzzled.

"You will know," Yoda answered. "When you are at peace . . . calm, passive. A Jedi uses the Force for knowledge. Never for attack."

"But tell me why—" Luke began.

"No! There is no why. Nothing more will I tell you. Clear your mind of questions. Quiet now be—at peace . . ." Yoda's voice trailed off, but his words had a hypnotic effect on Luke. The young student stopped protesting and began to feel peaceful, his body and mind relaxing.

"Yes . . ." Yoda murmured, "calm."

Slowly Luke's eyes closed as he let his mind clear of distracting thoughts.

"Passive . . ."

Luke heard Yoda's soothing voice as it entered the receptive darkness of his mind. He willed himself to travel along with the master's words to wherever they might lead.

"Let yourself go . . ."

When Yoda perceived that Luke was as relaxed as the young student could be at this stage, he made the tiniest of gestures. As he did, the two seeker balls above his head shot toward Luke, firing stun bolts as they moved.

In that instant Luke sprang to life and ignited his laser sword. He leaped to his feet and, with pure concentration, began deflecting the bolts as they spun toward him. Fearlessly he faced the attack, and moved and dodged with extreme grace. His leaps into the air, as he jumped to meet the bolts, were higher than any he had achieved before. Luke wasted not a single motion as he concentrated only on every bolt as it sped his way.

Then, as suddenly as it had begun, the seeker attack was over. The glowing balls returned to hover on either side of their master's head.

Artoo-Detoo, the ever-patient observer, let out an electronic sigh and shook his metal dome-head.

Grinning proudly, Luke looked toward Yoda.

"Much progress do you make, young one," the Jedi Master confirmed. "Stronger do you grow." But the little instructor would not compliment him more than that.

Luke was full of pride at his marvelous achievement. He watched Yoda, expectantly waiting for further praise from him. But Yoda did not move or speak. He sat calmly—and then two more seeker balls floated up behind him and moved into formation with the first two.

Luke Skywalker's grin began to melt away.

A pair of white-armored stormtroopers lifted Captain Needa's lifeless form from the floor of Darth Vader's Imperial Star Destroyer.

Needa had known that death was the likely consequence of his failure to capture the *Millennium Falcon*. He had known, too, that he had to report the situation to Vader and make his formal apology. But there was no mercy for failure among the Imperial military. And Vader, in disgust, had signaled for the captain's death.

The Dark Lord turned, and Admiral Piett and two of his captains came to report their findings. "Lord Vader," Piett said, "our ships have completed their scan of the area and found nothing. The *Millennium Falcon* definitely went into lightspeed. It's probably somewhere on the other side of the galaxy by now."

Vader hissed through his breath mask. "Alert all commands," he ordered. "Calculate every possible destination along their last known trajectory and disburse the fleet to search for them. Don't fail me again, Admiral, I've had quite enough!"

Admiral Piett thought of the *Avenger*'s captain, whom he had just seen carried out of the room like

a sack of grain. And he remembered the excruciating demise of Admiral Ozzel. "Yes, my lord," he
answered, trying to hide his fear. "We'll find them."

Then the admiral turned to an aide. "Deploy the
fleet," he instructed. As the aide moved to carry
out his orders, a shadow of worry crossed the admiral's face. He was not at all certain that his luck
would be any better than that of Ozzel or Needa.

Lord Vader's Imperial Star Destroyer regally
moved off into space. Its protecting fleet of smaller
craft hovered nearby as the Imperial armada left
the Star Destroyer *Avenger* behind.

No one on the *Avenger* or in Vader's entire fleet
had any idea how near they were to their prey. As
the *Avenger* glided off into space to continue its
search, it carried with it, clinging unnoticed to one
side of the huge bridge tower, a saucer-shaped
freighter ship—the *Millennium Falcon*.

Inside the *Falcon*'s cockpit all was quiet. Han
Solo had stopped his ship and shut down all systems
so quickly that even the customarily talkative See-
Threepio was silent. Threepio stood, not moving a
rivet, a look of wonder frozen on his golden face.

"You could have warned him before you shut
him off," Princess Leia said, looking at the droid
that stood motionless like a bronzed statue.

"Oh, so sorry!" Han said in mock concern.
"Didn't mean to offend your droid. You think brak-
ing and shutting everything down in that amount of
time is easy?"

Leia was dubious about Han's entire strategy.
"I'm still not sure what you've accomplished."

He shrugged off her doubt. She'll find out soon
enough, he thought; there just wasn't any other

choice. He turned to his copilot. "Chewie, check the manual release on the landing claws."

The Wookiee barked, then pulled himself out of his chair and moved toward the rear of the ship.

Leia watched as Chewbacca proceeded to disengage the landing claws so that the ship could take off without mechanical delay.

Shaking her head incredulously, she turned to Han. "What do you have in mind for your *next* move?"

"The fleet is finally breaking up," he answered as he pointed out a port window. "I'm *hoping* they follow standard Imperial procedure and dump their garbage before they go into light-speed."

The princess reflected on this strategy for a moment, and then began to smile. This crazy man might know what he was doing after all. Impressed, she patted him on the head. "Not bad, hot shot, not bad. Then what?"

"Then," Han said, "we have to find a safe port around here. Got any ideas?"

"That depends. Where are we?"

"Here," Han said, pointing to a configuration of small light points, "near the Anoat system."

Slipping out of her chair, Leia moved next to him for a better look at the screen.

"Funny," Han said after thinking for a moment, "I have the feeling I've been in this area before. Let me check my logs."

"You keep logs?" Leia was more impressed by the minute. "My, how organized," she teased.

"Well, sometimes," he answered as he hunted through the computer readout. "Ah-ha, I knew it! Lando—now this should be interesting."

"I never heard of that system," said Leia.

"It's not a system. He's a man, Lando Calrissian.

A gambler, con artist, all-around scoundrel," he paused long enough for the last word to sink in, and gave the princess a wink, ". . . your kind of guy. The Bespin system. It's a fair distance but reachable."

Leia looked at one of the computer monitor screens and read the data. "A mining colony," she noted.

"A Tibanna gas mine," Han added. "Lando won it in a sabacc match, or so he claims. Lando and I go way back."

"Can you trust him?" Leia asked.

"No. But he has no love for the Empire, that much I know."

The Wookiee barked over the intercom.

Quickly responding, Han flicked some switches to bring new information to the computer screens, and then stretched to look out the cockpit window. "I see it, Chewie, I see it," he said. "Prepare the manual release." Then, turning to the princess, Han said, "Here goes nothing, sweetheart." He leaned back in his chair and smiled invitingly at her.

Leia shook her head, then grinned shyly and gave him a quick kiss. "You do have your moments," she reluctantly admitted. "Not many, but you have them."

Han was getting used to the princess's left-handed compliments, and he couldn't say that he really minded them. More and more he was enjoying the fact that she shared his own sarcastic sense of humor. And he was fairly sure that she was enjoying it, too.

"Let 'er go, Chewie," he shouted gleefully.

The hatch on the underbelly of the *Avenger* yawned open. And as the Imperial galactic cruiser zoomed into hyperspace, it spewed out its own belt of artificial asteroids—garbage and sections of irreparable machinery that scattered out into the black void of space. Hidden among that trail of refuse, the *Millennium Falcon* tumbled undetected off the side of the larger ship, and was left far behind as the *Avenger* streaked away.

Safe at last, Han Solo thought.

The *Millennium Falcon* ignited its ion engines, and raced off through the train of drifting space junk toward another system.

But concealed among that scattered debris was another ship.

And as the *Falcon* roared off to seek the Bespin system, this other ship ignited its own engines. Boba Fett, the most notorious and dreaded bounty hunter in the galaxy, turned his small, elephant's head-shaped craft, *Slave I,* to begin its pursuit. For Boba Fett had no intention of losing sight of the *Millennium Falcon*. Its pilot had too high a price on his head. And this was one reward that the fearsome bounty hunter was quite determined to collect.

Luke felt that he was definitely progressing.

He ran through the jungle—with Yoda perched on his neck—and leaped with gazellelike grace over the profusion of foliage and tree roots growing throughout the bog.

Luke had at last begun to detach himself from the emotion of pride. He felt unburdened, and was finally open to experience fully the flow of the Force.

When his diminutive instructor threw a silver bar above Luke's head, the young Jedi student reacted instantly. In a flash he turned to slice the bar into four shiny segments before it fell to the ground.

Yoda was pleased and smiled at Luke's accomplishment. "Four this time! The Force you feel."

But Luke was suddenly distracted. He sensed something dangerous, something evil. "Something's not right," he said to Yoda. "I feel danger . . . death."

He looked around him, trying to see what it was that emitted so powerful an aura. As he turned he saw a huge, tangled tree, its blackened bark dry and crumbling. The base of the tree was surrounded by a small pond of water, where the gigantic roots had grown to form the opening to a darkly sinister cave.

Luke gently lifted Yoda from his neck and set him on the ground. Transfixed, the Jedi student stared at the dark monstrosity. Breathing hard, he found himself unable to speak.

"You brought me here purposely," Luke said at last.

Yoda sat on a tangled root and put his Gimer Stick in his mouth. Calmly looking at Luke, he said nothing.

Luke shivered. "I feel cold," he said, still gazing at the tree.

"This tree is strong with the dark side of the Force. A servant of evil it is. Into it you must go."

Luke felt a tremor of apprehension. "What's in there?"

"Only what you take with you," Yoda said cryptically.

Luke looked warily at Yoda, and then at the tree. He silently resolved to take his courage, his willingness to learn, and step within that darkness to face whatever it was that awaited him. He would take nothing more than—

No. He would also bring his lightsaber.

Lighting his weapon, Luke stepped through the shallow waters of the pond and toward the dark opening between those great and foreboding roots.

But the Jedi Master's voice stopped him.

"Your weapon," Yoda reproved. "You won't need it."

Luke paused and looked again at the tree. Go into that evil cave completely unarmed? As skilled as Luke was becoming, he did not feel quite equal to that test. He gripped his saber tighter and shook his head.

Yoda shrugged and placidly gnawed his Gimer Stick.

Taking a deep breath, Luke cautiously stepped into the grotesque tree cave.

The dark inside the cave was so thick that Luke could feel it against his skin, so black that the light thrown by his laser sword was quickly absorbed and illuminated scarcely more than a meter in front of him. As he slowly moved forward, slimy, dripping things brushed against his face and the moisture from the soggy cave floor began to seep into his boots.

As he pushed through the blackness, his eyes began to grow accustomed to the dark. He saw a corridor before him, but as he moved toward it, he was surprised by a thick, sticky membrane that completely enveloped him. Like the web of some gigantic spider, the mass clung tightly to Luke's body. Thrashing at it with his lightsaber, Luke finally managed to disentangle himself and clear a path ahead.

He held his glowing sword in front of him and noticed an object on the cave floor. Pointing his lightsaber downward, Luke illuminated a black, shiny beetle the size of his hand. In an instant, the thing scurried up the slimy wall to join a cluster of its mates.

Luke caught his breath and stepped back. At that moment he considered hunting for the exit—but he braced himself and ventured still deeper into the dark chamber.

He felt the space about him widen as he moved forward, using his lightsaber as a dim beacon. He strained to see in the darkness, trying his best to hear. But there was no sound at all. Nothing.

Then, a very loud *hiss*.

The sound was familiar. He froze where he stood. He had heard that hiss even in his nightmares; it was the labored breath of a thing that had once been a man.

Out of the darkness a light appeared—the blue flame of a just-ignited laser sword. In its illumination Luke saw the looming figure of Darth Vader raise his lighted weapon to attack, and then lunge.

Prepared by his disciplined Jedi training, Luke was ready. He raised his own lightsaber and perfectly side-stepped Vader's attack. In the same movement, Luke turned to Vader and, with his mind and body completely focused, the youth summoned the Force. Feeling its power within him, Luke raised his laser weapon and brought it crashing down on Vader's head.

With one powerful stroke, the Dark Lord's head was severed from his body. Head and helmet crashed to the ground and rolled about the cave floor with a loud metallic bang. As Luke watched in astonishment, Vader's body was completely swallowed up by the darkness. Then Luke looked down at the helmet that had come to rest directly in front of him. For a moment it was completely still. Then the helmet cracked in half and split open.

As Luke watched in shocked disbelief, the broken helmet fell aside to reveal, not the unknown, imagined face of Darth Vader, but Luke's own face, looking up at him.

He gasped, horrified at the sight. And then, as suddenly as it had appeared, the decapitated head faded away as if in a ghostly vision.

Luke stared at the dark space where the head and pieces of helmet had lain. His mind reeled, the emotions that raged inside of him were almost too much to bear.

The tree! he told himself. It was all some trick of this ugly cave, some charade of Yoda's, arranged because he had come into the tree carrying a weapon.

He wondered if he were really fighting himself, or if he had fallen prey to the temptations of the dark side of the Force. He might himself become a figure as evil as Darth Vader. And he wondered if there might be some even darker meaning behind the unsettling vision.

It was a long while before Luke Skywalker was able to move from that deep, dark cave.

Meanwhile, sitting on the root, the little Jedi Master calmly gnawed his Gimer Stick.

XI

IT was dawn on the gaseous Bespin planet.

As the *Millennium Falcon* began its approach through the planet's atmosphere, it soared past several of Bespin's many moons. The planet itself glowed with the same soft pink hue of dawn that tinted the hull of the powerful pirate starship. As the ship neared, it swerved to avoid a billowing canyon of clouds that swirled up around the planet.

When Han Solo finally lowered his ship through the clouds, he and his crew got their first glimpse of the gaseous world of Bespin. And as they maneuvered through the clouds, they noticed that they were being followed by some kind of flying vehicle. Han recognized the craft as a twin-pod cloud car but was surprised when the car began to bank close to his freighter. The *Falcon* suddenly lurched as a round of laser fire struck its hull. No one on the *Falcon* had expected *this* kind of greeting.

The other craft transmitted a static-obscured message over the *Falcon*'s radio system.

"No," Han snarled in reply, "I do not have a landing permit. My registration is—"

But his words were drowned out by a loud crackle of radio static.

The twin-pod car was apparently not willing to

accept static for a reply. Again it opened up fire on
the *Falcon,* shaking and rattling the ship with each
strike.

A clear warning voice came over the freighter's
speakers: "Stand by. Any aggressive move will
bring about your destruction."

At this point Han had no intention of making
any aggressive moves. Bespin was their only hope
of sanctuary, and he didn't plan to alienate his
prospective hosts.

"Rather touchy, aren't they?" the reactivated See-
Threepio asked.

"I thought you knew these people," Leia chided,
casting a suspicious look at Han.

"Well," the Corellian hedged, "it's been a
while."

Chewbacca growled and barked, shaking his
head meaningfully at Han.

"That was a long time ago," he answered sharply.
"I'm sure he's forgotten all about it." But he began
to wonder if Lando had forgotten the past . . .

"Permission granted to land on Platform 327.
Any deviation of flight pattern will bring about
your—"

Angrily, Han switched off the radio. Why was
he being put through this harrassment? He was
coming here peacefully; wasn't Lando going to let
bygones be bygones? Chewbacca grunted and
glanced at Solo, who turned to Leia and her worried robot. "He'll help us," he said, trying to reassure them all. "We go way back . . . really. Don't
worry."

"Who's worried?" she lied unconvincingly.

By then they could clearly see the Cloud City of
Bespin through the cockpit window. The city was
immense and seemed to float in the clouds as it

emerged through the white atmosphere. As the *Millennium Falcon* approached the city, it became evident that the expansive city structure was supported from below by a thin unipod. The base of this supporting stalk was a large round reactor that floated through its billowing sea of clouds.

The *Millennium Falcon* dipped closer to the huge city and veered in the direction of its landing platforms, flying past the rising towers and spires that dotted the city's landscape. In and about these structures cruised more of the twin-pod cloud cars, gliding effortlessly through the mists.

Han gently brought the *Falcon* in to land on Platform 327; and as the ship's ion engines whined to a stop, the captain and his crew could see the welcoming party moving toward the landing platform with weapons drawn. Like any cross-section of the citizenry of Cloud City, this group included aliens, droids, and humans of all races and descriptions. One of these humans was the group's leader, Lando Calrissian.

Lando, a handsome black man perhaps the same age as Solo, was clad in elegant gray pants, blue shirt, and a flowing blue cape. He stood, unsmiling, on Landing Platform 327, waiting for the *Falcon*'s crew to disembark.

Han Solo and Princess Leia appeared at the open door of their ship, with blasters drawn. Standing behind them was the giant Wookiee, his gun in hand and a bandoleer of ammunition packs slung over his left shoulder.

Han didn't speak but quietly surveyed the menacing welcoming party that was marching across the platform toward them. An early morning wind began to sweep along the ground, making Lando's cloak fly up behind him like enormous deep blue wings.

"I don't like this," Leia whispered to Han.

He didn't much like it either, but he wasn't going to let the princess know that. "It'll be all right," he said quietly. "Trust me." Then, cautioning her, he added, "But keep your eyes open. Wait here."

Han and Chewbacca left Leia guarding the *Falcon* and they walked down the ramp to face Calrissian and his motley army. The two parties moved toward each other until Han and Calrissian stopped, three meters apart, to face each other. For a long moment, each one eyed the other silently.

Finally Calrissian spoke, shaking his head and squinting at Han. "Why, you slimy, double-crossing, no-good swindler," he said grimly.

"I can explain everything, ol' buddy," Han said quickly, "if you'll just listen."

Still unsmiling, Lando surprised alien and human alike when he said, "Glad to see you."

Han lifted an eyebrow skeptically. "No hard feelings?"

"Are you kidding?" Lando asked coolly.

Han was becoming nervous. Had he been forgiven or not? The guards and aides still had not lowered their weapons, and Lando's attitude was mystifying. Trying to conceal his worry, Han remarked gallantly, "I always said you were a gentleman."

With that, the other man broke into a grin. "I'll bet," he chuckled.

Han laughed in relief, as the two old friends at last embraced each other like the long-lost accomplices they were.

Lando waved at the Wookiee, standing behind his boss. "How you doing, Chewbacca?" he asked amiably. "Still wasting your time with this clown, eh?"

The Wookiee growled a reserved greeting.

Calrissian was not certain what to make of that growl. "Right," he half-smiled, looking uncomfortable. But his attention was distracted from this shaggy mass of muscle and hair when he saw Leia beginning to walk down the ramp. This lovely vision was followed closely by her protocol droid, who cautiously glanced around as they walked toward Lando and Han.

"Hello! What have we here?" Calrissian welcomed her admiringly. "I am Lando Calrissian, administrator of this facility. And who might you be?"

The princess remained coolly polite. "You may call me Leia," she replied.

Lando bowed formally and gently kissed the princess's hand.

"And I," her robot companion said, introducing himself to the administrator, "am See-Threepio, human–cyborg relations, at your—"

But before Threepio could finish his little speech, Han draped one arm about Lando's shoulder and steered him away from the princess. "She's traveling with me, Lando," he advised his old friend, "and I don't intend to gamble her away. So you might as well forget she exists."

Lando looked longingly over his shoulder as he and Han began to walk across the landing platform, followed by Leia, Threepio, and Chewbacca. "That won't be easy, my friend," Lando said regretfully.

Then he turned to Han. "What brings you here anyway?"

"Repairs."

Mock panic spread across Lando's face. "What have you done to my ship?"

Grinning, Han glanced back at Leia. "Lando used to own the *Falcon*," he explained. "And he sometimes forgets that he lost her fair and square."

Lando shrugged as he conceded to Han's boastful claim. "That ship saved my life more than a few times. It's the fastest hunk of junk in the galaxy. What's wrong with her?"

"Hyperdrive."

"I'll have my people get to work on it right away," Lando said. "I hate the thought of the *Millennium Falcon* without her heart."

The group crossed the narrow bridge that joined the landing area to the city—and were instantly dazzled by its beauty. They saw numerous small plazas ringed by smooth-edged towers and spires and buildings. The structures that constituted Cloud City's business and residential sections were gleaming white, shining brightly in the morning sun. Numerous alien races made up the city's populace and many of these citizens leisurely walked through the spacious streets alongside the *Falcon* visitors.

"How's your mining operation going?" Han asked Lando.

"Not as well as I'd like," Calrissian answered. "We're a small outpost and not very self-sufficient. I've had supply problems of every kind and . . ." The administrator noticed Han's amused grin. "What's so funny?"

"Nothing." Then Han chuckled. "I never would have guessed that underneath that wild schemer I

knew was a responsible leader and businessman."
Grudgingly, Han had to admit that he was impressed. "You wear it well."

Lando looked at his old friend reflectively. "Seeing you sure brings back a few memories." He shook his head, smiling. "Yes, I'm *responsible* these days. It's the price of success. And you know what, Han? You were right all along. It's overrated."

Both burst out laughing, causing a head or two to turn as the group moved through the city walkways.

See-Threepio lagged a bit behind, fascinated by the bustling alien crowds in the Cloud City streets, the floating cars, the fabulous, fanciful buildings. He turned his head back and forth, trying to register it all in his computer circuits.

As the golden droid gawked at the new sights, he passed a door facing the walkway. Hearing it open, he turned to see a silver Threepio unit emerging and stopped to watch the other robot move away. While Threepio paused there, he heard a muffled beeping and whistling coming from behind the door.

He peeked in and saw a familiar-looking droid sitting in the anteroom. "Oh, an R2 unit!" he chirped in delight. "I'd almost forgotten what they sound like."

Threepio moved through the doorway and walked into the room. Instantly he sensed that he and the R2 unit were not alone. He threw his golden arms up in surprise, the expression of wonder on his gilded faceplate frozen in place. "Oh, my!" he exclaimed. "Those look like—"

As he spoke, a rocketing laser bolt crashed into his metal chest, sending him flying in twenty directions around the room. His bronzed arms and legs crashed against the walls and settled in a smoldering heap with the rest of his mechanical body.

Behind him, the door slammed shut.

Some distance away, Lando guided the small group into his hall of offices, pointing out objects of interest as they moved through the white corridors. None of them had noticed Threepio's absence as they walked along, discussing life in Bespin.

But Chewbacca suddenly stopped and curiously sniffed the air as he looked behind him. Then he shrugged his huge shoulders and continued to follow the others.

Luke was perfectly calm. Even his present position did not make him feel tense or strained or unsure, or any of the negative things he used to feel when he first attempted this feat. He stood, perfectly balanced on one hand. He knew the Force was with him.

His patient master, Yoda, sat calmly on the soles of Luke's upturned feet. Luke concentrated serenely on his task and all at once he lifted four fingers from the ground. His balance undisturbed, he held his upside-down position—on one thumb.

Luke's determination had made him a quick study. He was eager to learn and was undaunted by the tests Yoda had devised for him. And now he felt confident that when he finally left this planet, it would be as a full-fledged Jedi Knight prepared to fight only for the noblest of causes.

Luke was rapidly growing stronger with the Force and, indeed, was accomplishing miracles. Yoda grew more pleased with his apprentice's progress. Once, while Yoda stood watching nearby,

Luke used the Force to lift two large equipment cases and suspend them in midair. Yoda was pleased, but noticed Artoo-Detoo observing this apparent impossibility and emitting electronic beeps of disbelief. The Jedi Master raised his hand and, with the Force, lifted the little droid off the ground.

Artoo hovered, his baffled internal circuits and sensors trying to detect the unseen power that held him suspended in the air. And suddenly the invisible hand played still another joke on him: While hanging in midair, the little robot was abruptly turned upside down. His white legs kicked desperately and his dome head spun helplessly around. When Yoda finally lowered his hand, the droid, along with two supply cases, began to drop. But only the boxes smashed against the ground. Artoo remained suspended in space.

Turning his head, Artoo perceived his young master, standing with hand extended, preventing Artoo from a fatal tumble.

Yoda shook his head, impressed by his student's quick thinking and by his control.

Yoda sprang onto Luke's arm and the two of them turned back toward the house. But they had forgotten something: Artoo-Detoo was still hanging in the air, beeping and whistling frantically, trying to get their attention. Yoda was merely playing another joke on the fretful droid, and as Yoda and Luke strolled away, Artoo heard the Jedi Master's bell-like laugh float in gay peals behind him as the droid slowly lowered to the ground.

Some time later, as dusk crept through the dense foliage of the bog, Artoo was cleaning the X-wing's hull. Through a hose that ran from the pond to an orifice in his side, the robot sprayed down the ship with a powerful stream of water. And while he worked, Luke and Yoda sat in the clearing, Luke's eyes closed in concentration.

"Be calm," Yoda told him. "Through the Force things you will see: other places, other thoughts, the future, the past, old friends long gone."

Luke was losing himself as he concentrated on Yoda's words. He was becoming unaware of his body and let his consciousness drift with the words of his master.

"My mind fills with so many images."

"Control, control you must learn of what you see," the Jedi Master instructed. "Not easy, not fast."

Luke closed his eyes, relaxed, and began to free his mind, began to control the images. At last there was something, not clear at first, but something white, amorphous. Gradually the image cleared. It seemed to be that of a city, a city that perhaps floated in a billowing white sea.

"I see a city in the clouds," he finally said.

"Bespin," Yoda identified it. "I see it, too. Friends you have there, heh? Concentrate and see them you will."

Luke's concentration intensified. And the city in the clouds became clearer. As he concentrated he was able to see forms, familiar forms of people he knew.

"I see them!" Luke exclaimed, his eyes still shut. Then a sudden agony, of body and spirit, took hold of him. "They're in pain. They're suffering."

"It is the future you see," the voice of Yoda explained.

The future, Luke thought. Then the pain he had felt had not yet been inflicted on his friends. So perhaps the future was not unchangeable.

"Will they die?" he asked his master.

Yoda shook his head and shrugged gently. "Difficult to see. Always in motion is the future."

Luke opened his eyes again. He stood up and quickly began to gather his equipment. "They're my friends," he said, guessing that the Jedi Master might try to dissuade him from doing what he knew he must.

"And therefore," Yoda added, "decide you must how to serve them best. If you leave now, help them you could. But you would destroy all for which they have fought and suffered."

His words stopped Luke cold. The youth sank to the ground, feeling a shroud of gloom envelop him. Could he really destroy everything he had worked for and possibly also destroy his friends? But how could he *not* try to save them?

Artoo perceived his master's despair and rolled over to stand by him and provide what comfort he could.

Chewbacca, who had grown concerned about See-Threepio, slipped away from Han Solo and the others and began hunting for the missing droid. All he had to follow were his keen Wookiee instincts as he wandered through the unfamiliar white passageways and corridors of Bespin.

Following his senses, Chewbacca finally came upon an enormous room in a corridor on the outside of the Cloud City. He approached the entrance to the room and heard the clamor of metallic objects clattering together. Along with the clanging, he heard the low grunting of creatures he had never encountered before.

The room he had found was a Cloud City junk

room—the repository of all the city's broken machines and other discarded metal junk.

Standing amid the scattered pieces of metal and tangled wire were four hoglike creatures. White hair grew thickly on their heads and partially covered their wrinkled piggish faces. The humanoid beasts —called Ugnaughts on this planet—were busy separating the junked pieces of metal and casting them into a pit of molten metal.

Chewbacca entered the room and saw that one of the Ugnaughts held a familiar-looking piece of golden metal.

The piglike creature was already raising his arm to toss the severed metal leg into the sizzling pit when Chewbacca roared at him, barking desperately. The Ugnaught dropped the leg and ran, to cower in terror with his fellows.

The Wookiee grabbed the metal leg and inspected it closely. He hadn't been mistaken. And as he growled angrily at the huddled Ugnaughts, they shivered and grunted like a pack of frightened pigs.

Sunlight streamed into the circular lounge of the apartments assigned to Han Solo and his group. The lounge was white and furnished simply, with a couch and a table and little of anything else. Each of the four sliding doors, placed along the circular wall, led to an adjoining apartment.

Han leaned out the lounge's large bay window to take in the panoramic view of Cloud City. The sight was breathtaking, even to such a jaded star jockey. He watched the flying cloud cars weave between the towering buildings, then looked down to see the people moving through the networks of streets below. The cool, clean air swept against his face, and, at least for the present, he felt as if he didn't have a care in all the universe.

A door behind him opened, and he turned to see Princess Leia standing in the entranceway to her apartment. She was stunning. Dressed in red with a cloud-white cloak flowing to the floor, Leia looked more beautiful than Han had ever seen her. Her long, dark hair was tied with ribbons and it softly framed her oval face. And she was looking at him, smiling at his astounded expression.

"What are you staring at?" she asked, beginning to blush.

"Who's staring?"

"You look silly," she said, laughing.

"You look great."

Leia looked away in embarrassment. "Has Three-pio turned up yet?" she asked, trying to change the subject.

Solo was taken off guard. "Huh? Oh. Chewie went to look for him. He's been gone too long just to be lost." He patted the softly cushioned sofa. "Come over here," he beckoned. "I want to check this out."

She thought about his invitation for a moment, then walked over and sat next to him on the couch. Han was overjoyed at her apparent compliance and leaned over to put his arm around her. But just before he had quite succeeded, she spoke again. "I hope Luke made it to the fleet all right."

"Luke!" He was becoming exasperated. How hard did he have to play at this game of hard-to-get? It was her game, and her rules—but he *had* chosen to play. She was too lovely to resist. "I'm sure he's fine," Han said, soothingly. "Probably sitting around wondering what we're doing right now."

He moved closer and put his arm around her shoulders, pulling her closer to him. She gazed at him invitingly, and he moved to kiss her—

Just then one of the doors zapped open. Chewbacca lumbered in carrying a large packing case filled with disturbingly familiar metal parts—the remains, in bronzed bits and pieces, of See-Threepio. The Wookiee dropped the case on the table. Gesturing toward Han, he barked and growled in distress.

"What happened?" Leia asked, moving closer to inspect the pile of disjointed parts.

"He found Threepio in a junk room."

Leia gasped. "What a mess! Chewie, do you think you can repair him?"

Chewbacca studied the collection of robot parts, then, looking back at the princess, shrugged his shoulders and howled. It looked to him like an impossible job.

"Why don't we just turn him over to Lando to fix?" Han suggested.

"No thanks," Leia answered, with a cold look in her eyes. "Something's wrong here. Your friend Lando is very charming, but I don't trust him."

"Well, I do trust him," Han argued, defending his host. "Listen, sweetheart, I'm not going to have you accusing my friend of—"

But he was interrupted by a buzz as a door slid open, and Lando Calrissian entered the lounge. Smiling cordially, he walked toward the small group. "Sorry, am I interrupting anything?"

"Not really," the princess said distantly.

"My dear," Lando said, ignoring her coldness toward her, "your beauty is unparalleled. Truly you belong here with us among the clouds."

She smiled icily. "Thanks."

"Would you care to join me for a little refreshment?"

Han had to admit that he was a bit hungry. But for some reason he could not quite name, he felt a wave of suspicion about his friend flood over him. He didn't remember Calrissian being quite so polite, quite so smooth. Perhaps Leia was correct in her suspicions . . .

His thoughts were interrupted by Chewbacca's enthusiastic bark at the mention of food. The big Wookiee was licking his lips at the prospect of a hearty meal.

"Everyone's invited, of course," Lando said.

Leia took Lando's proffered arm and, as the group moved toward the door, Calrissian glimpsed the box of golden robot parts. "Having problems with your droid?" he asked.

Han and Leia exchanged a quick glance. If Han was going to ask for Lando's help in repairing the droid, now was the moment. "An accident," he grunted. "Nothing we can't handle."

They left the lounge, leaving behind them the shattered remains of the protocol droid.

The group strolled through the long white corridors and Leia walked between Han and Lando. Han wasn't at all certain he liked the prospect of competing with Lando for Leia's affections—especially under the circumstances. But they were dependent on Lando's good graces now. They had no other choice.

Joining them as they walked was Lando's personal aide, a tall bald man dressed in a gray jacket with ballooning yellow sleeves. The aide wore a radio device that wrapped around the back of his head and covered both his ears. He walked along with Chewbacca a short distance behind Han, Leia, and Lando, and as they walked toward Lando's dining hall, the administrator described the status of his planet's government.

"So you see," Lando explained, "we are a free station and do not fall under the jurisdiction of the Empire."

"You're part of the mining guild then?" Leia asked.

"Not actually. Our operation is small enough not to be noticed. Much of our trade is, well . . . unofficial."

They stepped onto a veranda that overlooked the spiraled top of Cloud City. From here they saw several flying cloud cars gracefully swooping around the beautiful spired buildings of the city. It was a spectacular view, and the visitors were very impressed.

"It's a lovely outpost," Leia marveled.

"Yes, we're proud of it," Lando replied. "You'll find the air quite special here . . . very stimulating." He smiled at Leia meaningfully. "You could grow to like it."

Han didn't miss Lando's flirtatious glance—and he didn't like it, either. "We don't plan on staying that long," he said brusquely.

Leia raised an eyebrow and glanced mischievously at the now-fuming Han Solo. "I find it most relaxing."

Lando chuckled, and led them from the veranda. They approached the dining hall with its massive closed doors and, as they paused in front of them, Chewbacca lifted his head and sniffed the air curiously. He turned and barked urgently at Han.

"Not now, Chewie," Han reproved, turning to

Calrissian. "Lando, aren't you afraid the Empire might eventually discover this little operation and shut you down?"

"That's always been the danger," the administrator replied. "It's loomed like a shadow over everything we've built here. But circumstances have developed which will insure security. You see, I've made a deal that will keep the Empire out of here forever."

With that the mighty doors slid open—and immediately Han understood just what that "deal" must have involved. At the far end of the huge banquet table stood the bounty hunter Boba Fett.

Fett stood next to a chair that held the black essence of evil itself—Darth Vader. Slowly the Dark Lord rose to his full, menacing two-meter height.

Han shot his meanest look at Lando.

"Sorry, friend," Lando said, sounding mildly apologetic. "I had no choice. They arrived right before you did."

"I'm sorry, too," Han snapped. In that instant, he cleared his blaster from its holster, aimed it directly at the figure in black, and began to pump laser bolts Vader's way.

But the man who may have been the fastest draw in the galaxy was not fast enough to surprise Vader. Before those bolts zipped halfway across the table, the Dark Lord had lifted a gauntlet-protected hand and effortlessly deflected them so they exploded against the wall in a harmless spray of flying white shards.

Astounded by what he had just seen, Han tried firing again. But before he could discharge another laser blast, something—something unseen yet incredibly strong—yanked the weapon from his hand and sent it flying into Vader's grip. The raven figure calmly placed the weapon on top of the dining table.

Hissing through his obsidian mask, the Dark Lord addressed his would-be assailant. "We would be honored if you joined us."

Artoo-Detoo felt the rain plunking on top of his metal dome as he trudged through the muddy puddles of the bog. He was headed for the sanctuary of Yoda's little hut, and soon his optical sensors picked up the golden glow shining through its windows. As he neared the inviting house, he felt a robot's relief that at last he would get out of this annoying, persistent rain.

But when he tried to pass through the entrance he discovered that his inflexible droid body just could not get in; he tried from one angle, then from another. At last the perception that he was simply the wrong shape to get in seeped into his computer mind.

He could scarcely believe his sensors. As he peered into the house, he scanned a busy figure, bustling about the kitchen, stirring steaming pots, chopping this and that, running back and forth. But the figure in Yoda's tiny kitchen, doing Yoda's kitchen tasks, was not the Jedi Master—but his apprentice.

Yoda, it appeared from Artoo's scan, was simply sitting back observing his young pupil from the adjacent room, and quietly smiling. Then suddenly, in the midst of all his kitchen activity, Luke paused, as if a painful vision had appeared before him.

Yoda noticed Luke's troubled look. As he watched his student, three glow-ball seekers appeared from behind Yoda and noiselessly shot through the air to attack the young Jedi from behind. Instantly Luke turned to face them, a pot lid in one hand and a spoon in the other.

The seekers sent one rocketing bolt after another directly at Luke. But, with astounding skill, he warded off every one. He knocked one of the seekers toward the open door where Artoo stood watching his master's performance. But the faithful droid saw the shining ball too late to avoid the bolt it shot at him. The impact knocked the shrieking robot onto the ground with a *clunk* that nearly shook loose his electronic insides.

Later that evening, after the student had successfully passed a number of his teacher's tests, a weary Luke Skywalker finally fell asleep on the ground outside Yoda's house. He slept fitfully, tossing and softly moaning. His concerned droid stood by him, reaching out an extension arm and covering Luke with the blanket that had slipped halfway off. But when Artoo started to roll away, Luke began to groan and shudder as if in the grip of some horrible nightmare.

Inside the house, Yoda heard the groans and hurried to his doorway.

Luke awoke from his sleep with a start. Dazed, he looked about him, then saw his teacher worriedly watching him from his house. "I can't keep the vision out of my head," Luke told Yoda. "My friends . . . they're in trouble . . . and I feel that—"

"Luke, you must not go," Yoda warned.

"But Han and Leia will die if I don't."

"You don't know that." It was the whispered voice of Ben, who was beginning to materialize before them. The dark-robed figure stood, a shimmering image, and told Luke, "Even Yoda cannot see their fate."

But Luke was deeply worried about his friends and was determined to do something. "I can help them!" he insisted.

"You're not ready yet," Ben said gently. "You still have much to learn."

"I feel the Force," Luke said.

"But you cannot control it. This is a dangerous stage for you, Luke. You are now most susceptible to the temptations of the dark side."

"Yes, yes," Yoda added. "To Obi-Wan you listen, young one. The tree. Remember your failure at the tree! Heh?"

Painfully, Luke remembered, though he felt he had gained a great deal of strength and understanding in that experience. "I've learned much since then. And I'll return to finish. I promise that, master."

"You underestimate the Emperor," Ben told him gravely. "It is you he wants. That is why your friends suffer."

"And that," Luke said, "is why I must go."

Kenobi was firm. "I will not lose you to the Emperor as I once lost Vader."

"You won't."

"Only a fully trained Jedi Knight, with the Force as his ally, will conquer Vader and his Emperor," Ben emphasized. "If you end your training now, if you choose the quick and easy path—as Vader did—you will become an agent of evil, and the galaxy will be plunged deeper into the abyss of hate and despair."

"Stopped they must be," Yoda interjected. "Do you hear? On this *all* depends."

"You are the last Jedi, Luke. You are our only hope. Be patient."

"And sacrifice Han and Leia?" the youth asked incredulously.

"If you honor what they fight for," Yoda said, pausing for a long moment, ". . . yes!"

Great anguish overcame Luke. He wasn't certain that he could reconcile the advice of these two great mentors with his own feelings. His friends were in terrible danger, and of course he must save them. But his teachers thought he was not ready, that he might be too vulnerable to the powerful Vader and his Emperor, that he might bring harm to his friends and himself—and possibly be lost forever on the path of evil.

Yet how could he fear these abstract things when Han and Leia were real and were suffering? How could he permit himself to fear possible danger to himself when his friends were presently in real danger of death?

There was no longer any question in his mind as to what he had to do.

It was dusk the next day on the bog planet when Artoo-Detoo settled himself into his nook behind the cockpit of Luke's X-wing fighter.

Yoda stood on one of the storage cases, watching Luke load the cases one by one into the fighter's underbelly as he worked in the glow of the X-wing's lights.

"I cannot protect you, Luke," the voice of Ben Kenobi came, as his robed figure took solid form. "If you choose to face Vader, you will do it alone. Once you've made this decision, I cannot interfere."

"I understand," Luke replied calmly. Then, turning to his droid, he said, "Artoo, fire up the power converters."

Artoo, who had already unfastened the power couplings on the ship, whistled happily, grateful to be leaving this dismal bog world, which was certainly no place for a droid.

"Luke," Ben advised, "use the Force only for knowledge and for defense, not as a weapon. Don't give in to hate or anger. They lead the way to the dark side."

Luke nodded, only half-listening. His mind was on the long journey and on the difficult tasks ahead of him. He must save his friends, whose lives were in danger because of him. He climbed into the cockpit, then looked at his little Jedi Master.

Yoda was deeply concerned about his apprentice. "Strong is Vader," he warned ominously. "Clouded is your fate. Mind what you have learned. Notice *everything, everything!* It can save you."

"I will, Master Yoda," Luke assured him. "I will and I'll be back to finish what I have begun. I give you my word!"

Artoo closed the cockpit and Luke started the engines.

Yoda and Obi-Wan Kenobi watched the X-wing gear its engines and begin to move away for takeoff.

"Told you, I did," Yoda said sorrowfully, as the sleek fighter craft began to lift into the misty heavens. "Reckless is he. Now things are going to worse."

"That boy is our last hope," Ben Kenobi said, his voice heavy with emotion.

"No," Kenobi's former teacher corrected with a knowing gleam in his large eyes, "there is another."

Yoda lifted his head toward the darkening sky where Luke's ship was already a barely distinguishable point of light among the flickering stars.

☐ XII

CHEWBACCA thought he was going mad!

The prison cell was flooded with hot, blinding light that seared his sensitive Wookiee eyes. Not even his huge hands and hairy arms, thrust up over his face, could entirely protect him from the glare. And to add to his misery, a high-pitched whistle blared into the cubicle, tormenting his keen sense of hearing. He roared in agony, but his guttural roars were drowned out by the piercing, screeching noise.

The Wookiee paced back and forth within the confines of the cell. Moaning pitifully, he pounded at the thick walls in desperation, wanting someone, anyone, to come and free him. While he pounded, the whistle that had nearly exploded his eardrums suddenly stopped and the deluge of light flickered and went out.

Chewbacca staggered back a step with the sudden absence of torture, and then moved to one of the cell walls to try to detect whether anyone was approaching to release him. But the thick walls revealed nothing and, maddened to a fury, Chewbacca slammed a giant fist against the wall.

But the wall stood undamaged and as impenetrable as before, and Chewbacca realized it would take more than Wookiee brute strength to topple it.

Despairing of his chances of breaking through the cell to freedom, Chewbacca shuffled toward the bed, where the box of 3PO parts had been placed.

Idly at first, and then with more interest, the Wookiee began poking through the box. It dawned on him that it might be possible to repair the disjointed droid. Not only would doing so pass the time, but it might be helpful to have Threepio back in working condition.

He picked up the golden head and gazed into its darkened eyes. He held the head and barked a few soliloquizing words as if to prepare the robot for the joy of re-entry into activity—or for the disappointment of Chewbacca's possible failure to reconstruct him properly.

Then, quite delicately for a creature of his size and strength, the giant Wookiee placed the staring head atop the bronzed torso. Tentatively he began experimenting with Threepio's tangle of wires and circuits. His mechanical skills had previously only been tested in repairs on the *Millennium Falcon,* so he wasn't at all certain he could complete the delicate task. Chewbacca jiggled and fiddled with the wires, baffled by this intricate mechanism, when suddenly Threepio's eyes lit up.

A whine came from inside the robot. It sounded vaguely like Threepio's normal voice, but was so low and so slow that the words were unintelligible.

"Imm-peeeeer-eee-all-storr-mmm-trppp . . ."

Bewildered, Chewbacca scratched his furry head and studied the broken robot intently. An idea came to him, and he tried switching one wire to another plug. Instantly Threepio began speaking in his normal voice. What he had to say sounded like words from a bad dream.

"Chewbacca!" the head of See-Threepio cried.

"Watch out, there are Imperial stormtroopers hidden in—" He paused, as if reliving the whole traumatic experience, and then he cried, "Oh, no! I've been shot!"

Chewbacca shook his head in sympathy. All he could do at this point was try to put the rest of See-Threepio back together again.

Quite possibly it was the first time Han Solo had ever screamed. Never had he endured such excruciating torment. He was strapped to a platform that angled away from the floor at approximately forty-five degrees. While he was strapped there, electric currents of searing power shot through his body at short intervals, each jolt more painfully powerful than the last. He squirmed to free himself but his agony was so severe that it was all he could do just to remain conscious.

Standing near the torture rack, Darth Vader silently watched Han Solo's ordeal. Seeming neither pleased nor displeased, he watched until he had seen enough, and then the Dark Lord turned his back on the writhing figure and left the cell, the door sliding behind him to muffle Solo's anguished screams.

Outside the torture chamber, Boba Fett waited for Lord Vader with Lando Calrissian and the administrator's aide.

With obvious disdain, Vader turned to Fett. "Bounty hunter," Vader addressed the man in the black-marked silver helmet, "if you are waiting for your reward, you will wait until I have Skywalker."

The self-assured Boba Fett appeared unruffled by this news. "I am in no hurry, Lord Vader. My concern is that Captain Solo not be damaged. The reward from Jabba the Hut is double if he's alive."

"His pain is considerable, bounty hunter," Vader hissed, "but he will not be harmed."

"What about Leia and the Wookiee?" Lando asked with some concern.

"You will find them well enough," Vader answered. "But," he added with unmistakable finality, "they must never again leave this city."

"That was never a condition of our agreement," Calrissian argued. "Nor was giving Han to this bounty hunter."

"Perhaps you think you're being treated unfairly," Vader said sarcastically.

"No," Lando said, glancing at his aide.

"Good," Vader continued, adding a veiled threat. "It would be most unfortunate if I had to leave a permanent garrison here."

Bowing his head reverently, Lando Calrissian waited until Darth Vader had turned and swept into a waiting elevator with the silver-armored bounty hunter. Then, taking his aide with him, the administrator of Cloud City strode swiftly down a white-walled corridor.

"This deal's becoming worse all the time," Lando complained.

"Maybe you should have tried to negotiate with him," the aide suggested.

Lando looked at his aide grimly. He was beginning to realize that the deal with Darth Vader was giving nothing to him. And, beyond that, it was bringing harm to people he might have called friends. Finally, he said, low enough not to be heard by any of Vader's spies, "I've got a bad feeling about this."

See-Threepio was at last beginning to feel something like his old self.

The Wookiee had been busily working on reconnecting the droid's many wires and internal circuits, and just now was beginning to figure out how to attach the limbs. So far he had reattached the head to the torso and had successfully completed connecting an arm. The rest of Threepio's parts still lay on the table with wires and circuits hanging out of the severed joints.

But, though the Wookiee was diligently working to complete his task, the golden droid began to complain vociferously. "Well, something's not right," he fussed, "because now I can't see."

The patient Wookiee barked, and adjusted a wire in Threepio's neck. At last the robot could see again and he breathed a little mechanical sigh of relief. "There now, that's better."

But it wasn't *much* better. When he cast his newly activated sensor gaze toward where his chest should be he saw—his back! "Wait—Oh, my. What have you done? I'm backwards!" Threepio sputtered. "You flea-bitten furball! Only an overgrown mophead like you would be stupid enough to put my head—"

The Wookiee growled menacingly. He had forgotten what a complainer this droid was. And this cell was too small for him to listen to any more of that! Before Threepio knew what was happening to him, the Wookiee lumbered over and pulled a wire. Instantly the grumbling ceased, and the room became quiet again.

Then there was a familiar scent nearing the cell.

The Wookiee sniffed the air and hurried to the door.

The cell door buzzed open and a ragged, exhausted Han Solo was shoved in by two Imperial stormtroopers. The troopers left and Chewbacca

quickly moved to his friend, embracing him with
relief. Han's face was pale, with dark circles under
his eyes. It seemed that he was on the verge of
collapse, and Chewbacca barked his concern to his
long-time companion.

"No," Han said wearily, "I'm all right. I'm all
right."

The door opened once again, and Princess Leia
was thrown into the cell by the stormtroopers. She
was still dressed in her elegant cloak but, like Han,
she looked tired and disheveled.

When the stormtroopers left and the door slid
shut behind them, Chewbacca helped Leia over to
Han. The two gazed at one another with great
emotion, then reached out and tightly embraced.
After a moment they kissed tenderly.

While Han still held her, Leia weakly asked him,
"Why are they doing this? I can't understand what
they're up to."

Han was as puzzled as she. "They had me howling on the scan grid, but they never asked me any
questions."

Then the door slid open again, admitting Lando
and two of his Cloud City guards.

"Get out of here, Lando!" Han snarled. If he
had felt stronger, he would have leaped up to attack his traitorous friend.

"Shut up a minute and listen," Lando snapped.
"I'm doing what I can to make this easier for you."

"This ought to be good," Han remarked causti-
cally.

"Vader has agreed to turn Leia and Chewie over
to me," explained Lando. "They'll have to stay
here, but at least they'll be safe."

Leia gasped. "What about Han?"

Lando looked solemnly at his friend. "I didn't

know you had a price on your head. Vader has given you to the bounty hunter."

The princess quickly looked at Han, concern flooding her eyes.

"You don't know much about much," Han said to Calrissian, "if you think Vader won't want us dead before all this is over."

"He doesn't want you all," Lando said. "He's after someone called Skywalker."

The two prisoners caught their breath at the casual mention of that name.

Han seemed puzzled. "Luke? I don't get it."

The princess's mind was racing. All the facts were beginning to fit together into a terrible mosaic. In the past, Vader had wanted Leia because of her political importance in the war between Empire and Rebel Alliance. Now she was almost beneath his notice, useful only for one possible function.

"Lord Vader has set a trap for him," Lando added, "and—"

Leia finished his statement. "We're the bait."

"All this just to get the kid?" Han asked. "What's so important about him?"

"Don't ask me, but he's on his way."

"Luke's coming here?"

Lando Calrissian nodded.

"You fixed us all pretty good," Han growled, spitting his words at Lando, "—friend!"

As he snarled that last, accusing word, Han Solo's strength returned in a rush. He put all of his might into a punch that sent Lando reeling. Instantly the two former friends were engaged in a furious, close-quarters battle. Lando's two guards moved closer to the two grappling opponents and began striking at Han with the butts of their laser rifles. One powerful blow struck Han on the chin and sent him flying across the room, blood streaming from his jaw.

Chewbacca began to growl savagely and started for the guards. As they raised their laser weapons, Lando shouted, "Don't shoot!"

Bruised and winded, the administrator turned to Han. "I've done what I can for you," he said. "I'm sorry it's not better, but I've got my own problems." Then turning to leave the cell, Lando Calrissian added, "I've already stuck my neck out farther than I should."

"Yeah," Han Solo retorted, regaining his composure, "you're a real hero."

When Lando had left with his guards, Leia and Chewbacca helped Han back to his feet and led him to one of the bunks. He eased his weary, battered body onto the bunk, and Leia took a piece of her cloak and began gently dabbing at his chin, cleaning off the oozing blood.

As she did so, she started to chuckle softly. "You certainly have a way with people," she teased.

Artoo-Detoo's head swiveled atop his barrellike body as his scanners perceived the star-studded void of the Bespin system.

The speeding X-wing had just entered the system, and was swooping through black space like a great white bird.

The R2 unit had a lot to communicate to his pilot. His electronic thoughts were tumbling out, one on top of the other, and were translated on the cockpit scope.

The grim-faced Luke quickly responded to the first of Artoo's urgent questions. "Yes," Luke replied. "I'm sure Threepio is with them."

The little robot whistled an excited exclamation. "Just hold on," Luke said patiently, "we'll be there soon."

Artoo's turning head perceived the regal clusters of stars, his innards warm and cheerful, as the X-wing continued like a celestial arrow toward a planet with a city in the clouds.

Lando Calrissian and Darth Vader stood near the hydraulic platform that dominated the huge carbon-freezing chamber. The Dark Lord was quiet while aides hurried to prepare the room.

The hydraulic platform was housed within a deep pit in the center of the chamber and was surrounded by countless steam pipes and enormous chemical tanks of varying shapes.

Standing guard with laser rifles clutched in their hands were four armor-suited Imperial stormtroopers.

Darth Vader turned to Calrissian after appraising the chamber. "The facility is crude," he remarked, "but it should suit our needs."

One of Vader's officers rushed to the Sith Lord's side. "Lord Vader," he reported, "ship approaching—X-wing class."

"Good," Vader said coldly. "Monitor Skywalker's progress and allow him to land. We'll have the chamber ready for him shortly."

"We only use this facility for carbon-freezing," the administrator of Cloud City said nervously. "If you put him in there, it might kill him."

But Vader had already considered that possibility. He knew a way to find out just how powerful this freezing unit was. "I don't wish the Emperor's prize to be damaged. We'll test it first." He caught the attention of one of his stormtroopers. "Bring in Solo," the Dark Lord commanded.

Lando quickly glanced at Vader. He hadn't been prepared for the pure evil that was manifested in this terrifying being.

The X-wing speedily made its descent, and began to pierce the dense cloud blanket enveloping the planet.

Luke checked his monitor screens with growing concern. Maybe Artoo had more information than he was getting on his own panel. He tapped out a question to the robot.

"You haven't picked up any patrol ships?"

Artoo-Detoo's reply was negative.

And so Luke, thoroughly convinced that his arrival was thus far undetected, pressed his ship onward, toward the city of his troubled vision.

Six of the piglike Ugnaughts frantically prepared the carbon-freezing chamber for use, while Lando Calrissian and Darth Vader—now the true master of Cloud City—observed the hasty activity.

As they scurried about the carbon-freezing platform, the Ugnaughts lowered a network of pipes—resembling some alien giant's circulatory system—into the pit. They raised the carbonite hoses and hammered them into place. Then the six humanoids lifted the heavy coffinlike container and set it securely onto the platform.

Boba Fett rushed in, leading a squad of six Imperial stormtroopers. The troopers shoved and pulled Han, Leia, and the Wookiee in front of them, forcing them to hurry into the chamber. Strapped to the Wookiee's broad back was the partially reassembled See-Threepio, whose unattached arm and legs were roughly bundled against his gilded torso. The droid's head, facing the opposite direction from Chewbacca's, frantically turned around to try to see where they were going and what lay in store for them.

Vader turned to the bounty hunter. "Put him in the carbon-freezing chamber."

"What if he doesn't survive?" the calculating Boba Fett asked. "He is worth a lot to me."

"The Empire will compensate you for the loss," Vader said succinctly.

Anguished, Leia protested, "No!"

Chewbacca threw back his maned head and gave out a bellowing Wookiee howl. Then he charged directly at the line of stormtroopers guarding Han.

Screaming in panic, See-Threepio raised his one functioning arm to protect his face.

"Wait!" the robot yelled. "What are you doing?"

But the Wookiee wrestled and grappled with the troopers, undaunted by their number or by Threepio's frightened shrieks.

"Oh, no . . . Don't hit me!" the droid begged, trying to protect his disassembled parts with his arm. "No! He doesn't mean it! Calm down, you hairy fool!"

More stormtroopers had come into the room and joined the fight. Some of the troopers began to club the Wookiee with the butts of their rifles, banging against Threepio in the process.

"Ouch!" the droid screamed. "*I* didn't do anything!"

The stormtroopers had begun to overpower Chewbacca, and were about to smash him in the face with their weapons when, over the sounds of the fray, Han shouted, "Chewie, no! Stop it, Chewbacca!"

Only Han Solo could deflect the maddened Wookiee from his battle. Straining against the hold of his guards, Han broke away from them and rushed over to break up the fight.

Vader signaled his guards to let Han go and signaled the battling stormtroopers to stop the fight.

Han gripped the massive forearms of his hairy friend to calm him down, then gave him a stern look.

The flustered Threepio was still fussing and fuming. "Oh, yes . . . stop, stop." Then, with a robotic sigh of relief, he said, "Thank heavens!"

Han and Chewbacca faced each other, the former looking grimly into his friend's eyes. For a moment they embraced tightly, then Han told the Wookiee, "Save your strength for another time, pal, when the odds are better." He mustered a reassuring wink, but the Wookiee was grief-stricken and barked a mournful wail.

"Yeah," Han said, trying his best to crack a grin, "I know. I feel the same way. Keep well." Han Solo turned to one of the guards. "You'd better chain him until it's over."

The subdued Chewbacca did not resist as the stormtrooper guards placed restraining bands around his wrists. Han gave his partner a final farewell hug, then turned to Princess Leia. He took her in his arms and they embraced as if they would never let go.

Then Leia pressed her lips to his in a lingering kiss of passion. When their kiss ended, tears were in her eyes. "I love you," she said softly. "I couldn't tell you before, but it's true."

He smiled his familiar cocky smile. "Just remember that, because I'll be back." Then his face grew tender and he kissed her gently on the forehead.

Tears began to roll down her cheeks as Han turned away from her and walked quietly and fearlessly toward the waiting hydraulic platform.

The Ugnaughts rushed to his side and positioned him on the platform, binding his arms and legs tightly onto the hydraulic deck. He stood alone and helpless, and gazed one last time at his friends. Chewbacca looked at his friend mournfully, Threepio's head peeking over the Wookiee's shoulder to get one last look at the brave man. The administrator, Calrissian, watched this ordeal, a solemn look of regret etched deeply into his face. And then there was Leia. Her face was contorted with the pain of her grief as she stood regally trying to be strong.

Leia's was the last face Han saw when he felt the hydraulic platform suddenly drop. As it dropped, the Wookiee bellowed a final, baleful farewell.

In that terrible moment, the grieving Leia turned away, and Lando grimaced in sorrow.

Instantly fiery liquid began to pour down into the pit in a great cascading shower of fluid and sparks.

Chewbacca half-turned from the horrifying spectacle, giving Threepio a better view of the process.

"They're encasing him in carbonite," the droid reported. "It's high-quality alloy. Much better than my own. He should be quite well protected . . . That is, if he survived the freezing process."

Chewbacca quickly glanced over his shoulder at Threepio, silencing his technical description with an angry bark.

When the liquid finally solidified, huge metal tongs lifted the smoldering figure from the pit. The figure, which was cooling rapidly, had a recognizably human shape, but was featureless and rocky like an unfinished sculpture.

Some of the hogmen, their hands protected by

thick black gloves, approached the metal-encased body of Han Solo and shoved the block over. After the figure crashed to the platform with a loud, metallic *clang,* the Ugnaughts hoisted it into the casket-shaped container. They then attached a boxlike electronic device to its side and stepped away.

Kneeling, Lando turned some knobs on the device and checked the gauge measuring the temperature of Han's body. He sighed with relief and nodded his head. "He's alive," he informed Han Solo's anxious friends, "and in perfect hibernation."

Darth Vader turned to Boba Fett. "He's all yours, bounty hunter," he hissed. "Reset the chamber for Skywalker."

"He's just landed, my lord," an aide informed him.

"See to it that he finds his way here."

Indicating Leia and Chewbacca, Lando told Vader, "I'll take what is mine now." He was determined to whisk them out of Vader's clutches before the Dark Lord reneged on their contract.

"Take them," Vader said, "but I'm keeping a detachment of troops here to watch over them."

"That wasn't part of the bargain," Lando protested hotly. "You said the Empire wouldn't interfere in—"

"I'm altering the bargain. Pray I don't alter it any further."

A sudden tightness grasped Lando's throat, a threatening sign of what would happen to him if he gave Vader any difficulty. Lando's hand automatically went to his neck, but in the next moment the unseen hold was released and the administrator turned to face Leia and Chewbacca. The look in his eyes might have expressed despair, but neither of them cared to look at him at all.

Luke and Artoo moved cautiously through a deserted corridor.

It concerned Luke that thus far they had not been stopped for questioning. No one had asked them for landing permits, identification papers, purpose of visit. No one in Cloud City seemed at all curious about who this young man and his little droid might be—or what they were doing there. It all seemed rather ominous, and Luke was beginning to feel very uneasy.

Suddenly he heard a sound at the far end of the corridor. Luke halted, pressing himself close against the corridor wall. Artoo, thrilled to think that they might be back among familiar droids and humans, began to whistle and beep excitedly. Luke glanced at him to be still, and the little robot emitted one last, feeble squeak. Luke then peered around a corner and saw a group approaching from a side hallway. Leading the group was an imposing figure in battered armor and helmet. Behind him, two Cloud City armed guards pushed a transparent case down the corridor. From where Luke stood it appeared the case contained a floating, statuelike human figure. Following the case were two Imperial stormtroopers, who spotted Luke.

Instantly, the troopers took aim and began to fire.

But Luke dodged their laser bolts and, before they could shoot another round, the youth fired his blaster, ripping two sizzling holes into the stormtroopers' armored chests.

As the troopers fell, the two guards quickly whisked the encased figure into another hallway and the armor-clad figure leveled his laser blaster at Luke, sending a deadly bolt at him. The beam just missed the youth, and nicked a large chunk out of the wall next to him, shattering it into a shower of dustlike particles. When the particles had cleared, Luke peeked back around the corner and saw that the nameless attacker, the guards, and the case had all disappeared behind a thick metal door.

Hearing sounds behind him, Luke turned to see Leia, Chewbacca, See-Threepio, and an unfamiliar man in a cloak moving down yet another hallway, and guarded by a small band of Imperial stormtroopers.

He gestured to catch the princess's attention.

"Leia!" he shouted.

"Luke, no!" she exclaimed, her voice charged with fear. "It's a trap!"

Leaving Artoo trailing behind, Luke ran off to follow them. But when he reached a small anteroom, Leia and the others had disappeared. Luke heard Artoo whistling frantically as he scooted toward the anteroom. Yet, as the youth swiftly turned, he saw a mammoth metal door crash down in front of the startled robot with a thundering *clang*.

With the slamming of that door, Luke was cut off from the main corridor. And, when he turned to find another way out, he saw more metal doors bang shut in the other doorways of the chamber.

Meanwhile, Artoo stood somewhat dazed by the shock of his close call. If he had rolled just a tiny bit farther into the anteroom, that door would have squashed him into scrap metal. He pressed his metal nose against the door, then gave out a whistle of relief and wandered off in the opposite direction.

The anteroom was full of hissing pipes and steam that belched from the floor. Luke began to explore the room and noticed an opening above his head, leading to a place he could not even imagine. He moved forward to get a better look, and as he did, the section of floor he stood on began to rise slowly upward. Luke rode up with the lifting platform, determined to face the foe he had traveled so far to meet.

Keeping his blaster clutched in his hand, Luke rose into the carbon-freezing chamber. The room was deathly quiet, except for the hissing of steam escaping some of the pipes in the room. It appeared to Luke that he was the only living creature in this chamber of strange machinery and chemical containers, but he sensed that he was not alone.

"Vader . . ."

He spoke the name to himself as he looked around the chamber.

"Lord Vader. I feel your presence. Show yourself," Luke taunted his unseen enemy, "or do you fear me?"

While Luke spoke, the escaping steam began to billow out in great clouds. Then, unaffected by the searing heat, Vader appeared and strode through the hissing vapors, stepping onto the narrow walkway above the chamber, his black cloak trailing behind him.

Luke took a cautious step toward the demonic figure in black and holstered his blaster. He experienced a surge of confidence and felt completely ready to face the Dark Lord as one Jedi against another. There was no need for his blaster. He sensed that the Force was with him and that, at last, he was ready for this inevitable battle. Slowly he began to mount the stairs toward Vader.

"The Force is with you, young Skywalker,"

Darth Vader said from above, "but you are not a Jedi yet."

Vader's words had a chilling effect. Briefly Luke hesitated, recalling the words of another former Jedi Knight: *"Luke, use the Force only for knowledge and for defense, not as a weapon. Don't give in to hate or anger. They lead the way to the dark side."*

But throwing aside any fragment of doubt, Luke gripped the smoothly finished handle of his lightsaber and quickly ignited the laser blade.

At the same instant, Vader ignited his own laser sword and quietly waited for the young Skywalker to attack.

His great hatred for Vader impelled Luke to lunge at him savagely, bringing his sizzling blade down upon Vader's. But effortlessly, the Dark Lord deflected the blow with a defensive turn of his own weapon.

Again Luke attacked. Once again their energy blades clashed.

And then they stood, staring at one another for an endless moment through their crossed lightsabers.

XIII

SIX Imperial stormtroopers guarded Lando, Leia, and Chewbacca as they marched through the inner corridor of Cloud City. They reached an intersection when twelve of Lando's guards, and his aide, arrived to block their path.

"Code Force Seven," Lando commanded as he stopped in front of his aide.

At that moment the twelve guards aimed their laser weapons at the startled stormtroopers, and Lando's aide calmly took the six troopers' weapons from them. He handed one of the guns to Leia and one to Lando, then waited for the next order.

"Hold them in the security tower," the Cloud City administrator said. "Quietly! No one must know."

The guards and Lando's aide, carrying the extra weapons, marched the stormtroopers away to the tower.

Leia had watched this rapid turn of events in confusion. But her confusion turned to astonishment when Lando, the man who had betrayed Han Solo, began removing Chewbacca's bonds.

"Come on," he urged. "We're getting out of here."

The Wookiee's giant hands were freed at last. Not caring to wait for explanations, Chewbacca turned toward the man who had freed him, and with a blood-curdling roar, lunged at Lando and began to throttle him.

"After what you did to Han," Leia said, "I wouldn't trust you to—"

Lando, desperately trying to free himself from Chewbacca's ferocious grip, tried to explain. "I had no choice," he began—but the Wookiee interrupted him with an angry bark.

"There's still a chance to save Han," Lando gasped. "They're at the East Platform."

"Chewie," Leia said at last, "let go!"

Still fuming, Chewbacca released Lando and glared at him as Calrissian fought to regain his breath.

"Keep your eyes on him, Chewie," Leia cautioned as the Wookiee growled threateningly.

"I have a feeling," Lando muttered under his breath, "that I'm making another big mistake."

The stout little R2 unit meandered up and down the corridor, sending his scanners in every possible direction as he tried to detect some sign of his master—or of *any* kind of life. He realized he was dreadfully turned around and had lost track of how many meters he had traveled.

As Artoo-Detoo turned a corner he spotted a number of forms moving up the corridor. Beeping and whistling droid greetings, he hoped that these were friendly sorts.

His tooting was detected by one of the creatures, who began to call out to him.

"Artoo . . . Artoo . . ." It was Threepio!

Chewbacca, still carrying the semiassembled

See-Threepio, quickly turned around to see the stubby R2 droid rolling their way. But as the Wookiee turned, Threepio was spun out of sight of his friend.

"Wait!" the aggravated Threepio demanded. "Turn around, you woolly . . . Artoo, hurry! We're trying to save Han from the bounty hunter."

Artoo scooted forward, beeping all the way, and Threepio patiently replied to his frantic questions. "I know. But Master Luke can take care of himself." At least that was what See-Threepio kept telling himself as the group continued its search for Han.

On the East Landing Platform of Cloud City, two guards shoved the frozen body of Han Solo through a side hatchway of the *Slave I*. Boba Fett climbed up a ladder next to the opening and boarded his ship, ordering it sealed as soon as he entered the cockpit.

Fett ignited his ship's engines and the craft began rolling across the platform for takeoff.

Lando, Leia, and Chewbacca raced onto the platform in time only to see the *Slave I* lifting off and soaring into the orange and purple of the Cloud City sunset. Raising his blaster, Chewbacca howled and fired the weapon at the departing spaceship.

"It's no use," Lando told him. "They're out of range."

All but Threepio gazed at the departing craft. Still strapped to Chewbacca's back, he saw something that the others had not yet noticed.

"Oh, my, no!" he exclaimed.

Charging the group was a squad of Imperial stormtroopers, blasts already issuing from their drawn blasters. The first bolt narrowly missed Princess Leia. Lando responded quickly in returning the enemy fire, and the air was ablaze with a brilliant criss-cross of red and green laser bolts.

Artoo scooted over to the platform's elevator and hid inside, peeking out to see the fury of the battle from a safe distance.

Lando shouted above the sounds of the blasters. "Come on, let's move!" he called, breaking for the open elevator and blasting at the stormtroopers as he ran.

But Leia and Chewbacca did not move. They stood their ground and kept up a steady fire against the assault of the stormtroopers. Troopers groaned and dropped as their chests, arms, and stomachs erupted under the fatally accurate aim of this one female human and one male Wookiee.

Lando, sticking his head out of the elevator, tried to get their attention, motioning them to run. But the two seemed possessed as they blasted away, getting retaliation for all of their anger and captivity and the loss of one they both loved. They were determined to extinguish the lives of these minions of the Galactic Empire.

Threepio would gladly have been *anywhere* else. Unable to get away, all he could do was frantically yell for help. "Artoo, help me!" he screamed. "How did I get into this? What a fate worse than death it is to be strapped to the back of a Wookiee!"

"Get in here!" Lando shouted again. "Hurry up! Hurry up!"

Leia and Chewbacca began to move toward him, evading the erupting rain of laser fire as they rushed inside the waiting elevator. As the elevator doors closed, they glimpsed the remaining troopers racing at them.

Lightsabers clashed in Luke Skywalker and Darth Vader's battle on the platform above the carbon-freezing chamber.

Luke felt the shaking platform shudder with every blow and parry and thrust of their weapons. But he was undaunted, for with every thrust of his sword he drove the evil Darth Vader back.

Vader, using his lightsaber to ward off Luke's aggressive lunges, spoke calmly as they fought. "The fear does not reach you. You have learned more than I anticipated."

"You'll find I'm full of surprises," the confident youth retorted, threatening Vader with yet another thrust.

"And I, too," was the calm, portentous reply.

With two graceful moves, the Dark Lord hooked Luke's weapon out of his hands and sent it flying away. A slash of Vader's energy blade at Luke's feet made the youth jump back in an effort to protect himself. But he stumbled backward, and tumbled down the stairs.

Sprawled on the platform, Luke gazed up and saw the ominous dark figure looming above him at the top of the stairs. Then the figure flew right at him, its sable cloak billowing out in the air like the wings of a monstrous bat.

Quickly Luke rolled to one side, not taking his eyes off Vader, as the vast black figure landed soundlessly next to him.

"Your future lies with me, Skywalker," Vader hissed, looming over the crouching youth. "Now you will embrace the dark side. Obi-Wan knew this to be true."

"No!" Luke yelled, trying to fight off the evil presence.

"There is much Obi-Wan did not tell you," Vader continued. "Come, I will complete your training."

Vader's influence was incredibly strong; it seemed to Luke like a thing alive.

Don't listen to him, Luke told himself. *He is trying to trick me, to lead me astray, to lead me to the dark side of the Force, just like Ben warned me!*

Luke began to back away from the advancing Sith Lord. Behind the youth, the hydraulic elevator cover silently opened, ready to receive him.

"I'll die first," Luke proclaimed.

"That won't be necessary." The Dark Lord suddenly lunged at Luke with his lightsaber, so forcefully that the youth lost his balance and tumbled into the gaping opening.

Vader turned away from the freezing-pit and casually deactivated his lightsaber. "All too easy," he shrugged. "Perhaps you are not as strong as the Emperor thought."

As he spoke, molten metal began to pour into the opening behind him. And, while his back was still turned, something rose in a blur upward.

"Time will tell," Luke quietly replied to Vader's remark.

The Dark Lord spun around. At this point in the freezing process, the subject certainly shouldn't be able to speak! Vader glanced around the room and then turned his helmeted head up toward the ceiling.

Hanging from some hoses draped across the ceiling, Luke was suspended, having leaped some five meters into the air to escape the carbonite.

"Impressive," Vader admitted, "your agility is impressive."

Luke dropped back to the platform on the other side of the steaming pit. He reached his hand out and his sword, lying on another part of the platform, flew back into his grip. Immediately the lightsaber ignited.

Vader's sword sprang to life at the very same moment. "Ben has taught you well. You have controlled your fear. Now release your anger. I destroyed your family. Take your revenge."

But this time Luke was cautious and more controlled. If he could subdue his anger, as he had finally controlled his fear, he would not be swayed.

Remember the training, Luke cautioned himself. *Remember what Yoda taught! Cast out all hatred and anger and receive the Force!*

Gaining control over his negative feelings, Luke began to advance, ignoring Vader's goading. He lunged at Vader and, after a quick exchange, began to force him back.

"Your hatred can give you the power to destroy me," Vader tempted. "Use it."

Luke began to realize just how awesomely powerful his dark enemy was, and softly told himself, "I will not become a slave to the dark side of the Force," and moved cautiously toward Vader.

As Luke approached, Vader slowly moved backward in retreat. Luke lunged at him with a powerful swing. But when Vader blocked it, he lost his balance and fell into the outer rim of steaming pipes.

Luke's knees nearly buckled with the exhaustion of battling his fearsome opponent. He gathered his strength and cautiously moved to the edge and looked down. But he saw no sign of Vader. Switching off his lightsaber and hooking it into his belt, Luke lowered himself into the pit.

He dropped to the floor of the pit and found himself in a large control and maintenance room that overlooked the reactor powering the entire city. Looking around the chamber, he noticed a large window; standing silhouetted in front of it was the unmoving figure of Darth Vader.

Luke slowly moved closer to the window and re-ignited his lightsaber.

But Vader did not light his own sword, nor did he make any effort to defend himself as Luke drew nearer. The Dark Lord's only weapon, in fact, was his tempting voice. "Attack," he goaded the young Jedi. "Destroy me."

Confused by Vader's ploy, Luke hesitated.

"Only by taking your revenge can you save yourself . . ."

Luke stood locked in place. Should he act on Vader's words and thus use the Force as a tool of revenge? Or should he step away from this battle now, hoping for another chance to fight Vader when he had gained better control?

No, how could he delay the opportunity to destroy this evil being? Here was his chance, now, and he must not delay . . .

There might never again be such an opportunity!

Luke grasped his deadly lightsaber in both hands, tightly gripping the smooth handle like an ancient broadsword and raising the weapon to deliver the blow that would slay this masked horror.

But before he could swing, a large piece of machinery detached itself from the wall behind him and came hurtling at his back. Turning instantly, Luke flashed his lightsaber and cut the thing in

half, and the two massive pieces crashed to the
floor.

A second piece of machinery sped toward the
youth, and he again used the Force to deflect it.
The weighty object bounced away as if it had
struck an unseen shield. Then a large pipe came
tumbling toward him through the air. But even
as Luke repelled that enormous object, tools and
pieces of machinery came flying at him from all
directions. Then wires, that pulled themselves out
of the walls, came twisting and sparking and
whipping at him.

Bombarded on all sides, Luke did what he
could to deflect the assault; but he was beginning
to get bloodied and bruised in the attempt.

Another large piece of machinery glanced off
Luke's body and crashed out the large window,
letting in the screaming wind. Suddenly everything
in the room was blown about, and the fierce wind
lashed Luke's body and filled the room with a
bansheelike howl.

And in the very center of the room, standing still
and triumphant, was Darth Vader.

"You are beaten," the Dark Lord of the Sith
gloated. "It is useless to resist. You will join me
or you will join Obi-Wan in death!"

As Vader spoke those words, a final piece of
heavy machinery soared through the air, striking
the young Jedi and knocking him through the
broken window. Everything became a great blur
as the wind carried him, tossing and rolling, until
he managed to grab hold of a beam with one hand.

When the wind subsided a bit and his vision
cleared, Luke realized that he was hanging from
the gantry of the reactor shaft outside the control

room. When he gazed down he saw what appeared to be an endless abyss. A wave of dizziness swept over him and he squeezed his eyes closed in an effort to keep from panicking.

Compared to the podlike reactor from which he hung, Luke was no more than a speck of squirming matter, while the pod itself—just one of many jutting from the circular, light-dotted inner wall—was no more than a speck itself in comparison with the rest of the immense chamber.

Grasping the beam firmly with only one hand, Luke managed to hook his lightsaber on to his belt and then grab the beam with both hands. Hoisting himself up, he scrambled onto the gantry and stood on it, just in time to see Darth Vader walking toward him down the shaft.

As Vader approached Luke, the public address system began to blare, echoing through the cavernous rooms: "Fugitives heading toward Platform 327. Secure all transports. All security forces on alert."

Walking menacingly toward Luke, Vader predicted, "Your friends will never escape and neither will you."

Vader took another step, and Luke immediately raised his sword, ready to renew the battle.

"You are beaten," Vader stated with horrifying certainty and finality. "It is useless to resist."

But Luke did resist. He lunged at the Dark Lord with a vicious blow, bringing his sizzling laser blade to crash onto Vader's armor and sear through to the flesh. Vader staggered from the blow, and it seemed to Luke that he was in pain. But only for a moment. Then, once again, Vader began to move toward him.

Taking another step, the Dark Lord warned,

"Don't let yourself be destroyed as Obi-Wan was."

Luke was breathing hard, cold sweat dropping from his forehead. But the sound of Ben's name instilled a sudden resolve in him.

"Calm—" he reminded himself. "Be calm."

But the grimly cloaked specter stalked toward him along the narrow gantry, and it seemed he wanted the young Jedi's life.

Or worse, his fragile soul.

Lando, Leia, Chewbacca, and the droids hurried down a corridor. They turned a corner and saw the door to the landing platform standing open. Through it they glimpsed the *Millennium Falcon* waiting for their escape. But suddenly the door slammed shut. Ducking into an alcove, the group saw a squad of stormtroopers charging them, their laser guns blasting as they ran. Chunks of wall and floor shattered and flew into the air with the impact of the ricocheting energy beams.

Chewbacca growled, returning the stormtroopers' fire with savage Wookiee rage. He covered Leia, who punched desperately at the door's control panel. But the door failed to budge.

"Artoo!" Threepio called. "The control panel. You can override the alert system."

Threepio gestured at the panel, urging the little robot to hurry, and pointing out a computer socket on the control board.

Artoo-Detoo scooted toward the control panel, beeping and whistling as he scurried to help.

Twisting his body to avoid the burning laser bolts, Lando feverishly worked to connect his comlink to the panel's intercom.

"This is Calrissian," he broadcast over the system. "The Empire is taking control of the city. I advise you to leave before more Imperial troops arrive."

He switched off the communicator. Lando knew that he had done what he could to warn his people; his job now was to get his friends safely off the planet.

Meanwhile, Artoo removed a connector cover and inserted an extended computer arm into the waiting socket. The droid issued a short beep that suddenly turned into a wild robot scream. He began to quiver, his circuits lighting up in a mad display of flashing brilliance, and every orifice in his hull spewing smoke. Lando quickly pulled Artoo away from the power socket. As the droid began to cool off, he directed a few wilted beeps Threepio's way.

"Well, next time *you* pay more attention," Threepio replied defensively. "I'm not supposed to know power sockets from computer feeds. I'm an interpreter—"

"Anybody else got any ideas?" Leia shouted as she stood firing at the attacking stormtroopers.

"Come on," Lando answered over the din of the battle, "we'll try another way."

The wind that shrieked through the reactor shaft entirely absorbed the sounds of the clashing lightsabers.

Luke moved agilely across the gantry and took refuge beneath a huge instrument panel to evade his pursuing foe. But Vader was there in an instant, his lightsaber thrashing down like a pulsating guillotine blade, cutting the instrument complex loose. The complex began to fall, but was abruptly caught by the wind and blown upward.

An instant of distraction was all Vader needed. As the instrument panel floated away, Luke involuntarily glanced at it. At that second, the Dark Lord's laser blade came slashing down across Luke's hand, cutting it, and sending the youth's lightsaber flying.

The pain was excruciating. Luke smelled the terrible odor of his own seared flesh and squeezed his forearm beneath his armpit to try to stop the agony. He stepped backward along the gantry until he reached its extreme end, stalked all the while by the black-garbed apparition.

Abruptly, ominously, the wind subsided. And Luke realized he had nowhere else to go.

"There is no escape," the Dark Lord of the Sith warned, looming over Luke like a black angel of death. "Don't make me destroy you. You are strong with the Force. Now you must learn to use the dark side. Join me and together we will be more powerful than the Emperor. Come, I will complete your training and we will rule the galaxy together."

Luke refused to give in to Vader's taunts. "I will never join you!"

"If you only knew the power of the dark side," Vader continued. "Obi-Wan never told you what happened to your father, did he?"

Mention of his father aroused Luke's anger. "He told me enough!" he yelled. "He told me you killed him."

"No," Vader replied calmly. "I am your father."

Stunned, Luke stared with disbelief at the black-clad warrior and then pulled away at this revelation. The two warriors stood staring at one another, father and son.

"No, no! That's not true . . ." Luke said, refusing to believe what he had just heard. "That's impossible."

"Search your feelings," Vader said, sounding like an evil version of Yoda, "you know it to be true."

Then Vader turned off the blade of his lightsaber and extended a steady and inviting hand.

Bewildered and horror-stricken at Vader's words, Luke shouted, "No! No!"

Vader continued persuasively. "Luke, you can destroy the Emperor. He has foreseen this. It is your destiny. Join me and together we can rule the galaxy as father and son. Come with me. It is the only way."

Luke's mind whirled with those words. Everything was finally beginning to coalesce in his brain. Or was it? He wondered if Vader were telling him the truth—if the training of Yoda, the teaching of saintly old Ben, his own strivings for good and his abhorrence of evil, if everything he had fought for were no more than a lie.

He didn't want to believe Vader, tried convincing himself that it was Vader who lied to him—but somehow he could *feel* the truth in the Dark Lord's words. But, if Darth Vader did speak the truth, why, he wondered, had Ben Kenobi lied to him? *Why?* His mind screamed louder than any wind the Dark Lord could ever summon against him.

The answers no longer seemed to matter.

His Father.

With the calmness that Ben himself and Yoda, the Jedi Master, had taught him, Luke Skywalker made, perhaps, what might be his final decision of all. "Never," Luke shouted as he stepped out into the empty abyss beneath him. For all its unperceived depth, Luke might have been falling to another galaxy.

Darth Vader moved to the end of the gantry to watch as Luke tumbled away. A strong wind began to blow, billowing Vader's black cloak out behind him as he stood looking over the edge.

Skywalker's body quickly plunged downward. Toppling head over foot, the wounded Jedi desperately reached out to grab at something to stop his fall.

The Dark Lord watched until he saw the youth's body sucked into a large exhaust pipe in the side of the reactor shaft. When Luke vanished, Vader quickly turned and hurried off the platform.

Luke sped through the exhaust shaft trying to grab the sides to slow his fall. But the smooth, shiny sides of the pipe had no hand-holes or ridges for Luke to grasp.

At last he came to the end of the tunnellike pipe, his feet striking hard against a circular grill. The grill, which opened over an apparently bottomless drop, was knocked out by the impact of Luke's momentum, and he felt his body start to slide out through the opening. Frantically clawing at the smooth interior of the pipe, Luke began to call out for assistance.

"Ben . . . Ben, help me," he pleaded desperately.

Even as he called out, he felt his fingers slip along the inside of the pipe, while his body inched ever closer to the yawning opening.

Cloud City was in chaos.

As soon as Lando Calrissian's broadcast was heard throughout the city, its residents began to panic. Some of them packed a few belongings, others just rushed out into the streets seeking escape. Soon the streets were filled with running humans and aliens, rushing chaotically through the city. Imperial stormtroopers charged after the fleeing inhabitants, exchanging laser fire with them in a raging, clamorous battle.

In one of the city's central corridors, Lando, Leia, and Chewbacca held off a squad of stormtroopers by blasting heavy rounds of laser bolts at the Imperial warriors. It was urgent that Lando and the others hold their ground, for they had come upon another entrance that would lead them to the landing platform. If only Artoo succeeded in opening the door.

Artoo was trying to remove the plate from this door's control panel. But because of the noise and distraction of the laser fire blasting around him, it was difficult for the little droid to concentrate on his work. He beeped to himself as he worked, sounding a bit befuddled to Threepio.

"What are you talking about?" Threepio called to him. "We're not interested in the hyperdrive on the *Millennium Falcon*. It's fixed. Just tell the computer to open the door."

Then, as Lando, Leia, and the Wookiee edged toward the door, dodging heavy Imperial laser fire, Artoo beeped triumphantly and the door snapped open.

"Artoo, you did it!" Threepio exclaimed. The droid would have applauded had his other arm been attached. "I never doubted you for a second."

"Hurry," Lando shouted, "or we'll never make it."

The helpful R2 unit came through once again. As the others dashed through the entrance, the stout robot sprayed out a thick fog—as dense as the clouds surrounding this world—that obscured his friends from the encroaching stormtroopers. Before the cloud had cleared, Lando and the others were racing toward Platform 327.

The stormtroopers followed, blasting at the small band of fugitives bolting toward the *Millennium Falcon*. Chewbacca and the robots boarded the freighter while Lando and Leia covered them with their blasters, cutting down still more of the Emperor's warriors.

When the low-pitched roar of the *Falcon*'s engines started and then rose to an ear-battering whine, Lando and Leia discharged a few more bolts of brilliant energy. Then they sprinted up the ramp. They entered the pirate ship and the main hatchway closed behind them. And as the ship began to move, they heard a barrage of Imperial laser fire that sounded as if the entire planet were splitting apart at its foundations.

Luke could no longer slow his inexorable slide out the exhaust pipe.

He slid the final few centimeters and then dropped through the cloudy atmosphere, his body spinning and his arms flailing to grip on to something solid.

After what seemed like forever, he caught hold of an electronic weather vane that jutted out from the bowllike underside of Cloud City. Winds buffeted him and clouds swirled around him as he held on tightly to the weather vane. But his strength was beginning to fail; he didn't think he could hang like this—suspended above the gaseous surface—for very much longer.

All was very quiet in the *Millennium Falcon* cockpit.

Leia, just catching her breath from their close escape, sat in Han Solo's chair. Thoughts of him rushed to her mind, but she tried not to worry about him, tried not to miss him.

Behind the princess, looking over her shoulder out the front windscreen, stood a silent and exhausted Lando Calrissian.

Slowly the ship began to move, picking up speed as it coursed along the landing platform.

The giant Wookiee, in his old copilot's chair, threw a series of switches that brought a dancing array of lights across the ship's main control panel. Pulling the throttle, Chewbacca began to guide the ship upward, to freedom.

Clouds rushed by the cockpit windows and everyone finally breathed with relief as the *Millennium Falcon* soared into a red-orange twilight sky.

Luke managed to hook one of his legs over the electronic weather vane, which continued to support his weight. But air from the exhaust pipe rushed at him, making it difficult for him to keep from slipping off the vane.

"Ben . . ." he moaned in agony. ". . . Ben."

Darth Vader strode onto the empty landing platform and watched the speck that was the *Millennium Falcon* disappear in the far distance.

He turned to his two aides. "Bring my ship in!" he commanded. And then he left, black robes flowing behind him, to prepare for his journey.

Somewhere near the supporting stalk of Cloud City, Luke spoke again. Concentrating his mind on one whom he thought cared for him and might somehow come to his aid, he called, "Leia, hear me." Pitifully he cried out once again. "Leia."

Just then, a large piece of the weather vane broke off and went hurtling off into the clouds far below. Luke tightened his grip on what remained of the vane, and strained to hold on in the blast of air rushing at him from the pipe above.

"It looks like three fighters," Lando said to Chewbacca as they watched the computer-screen configurations. "We can outdistance them easily," he added, knowing the capabilities of the freighter as well as Han Solo did.

Looking at Leia, he mourned the passing of his administratorship. "I knew that setup was too good to last," he moaned. "I'm going to miss it."

But Leia seemed to be in a daze. She didn't acknowledge Lando's comments, but stared straight ahead of her as if transfixed. Then, out of her dreamlike trance, she spoke. "Luke?" she said, as if responding to something she heard.

"What?" Lando asked.

"We've got to go back," she said urgently. "Chewie, head for the bottom of the city."

Lando looked at her in astonishment. "Wait a minute. We're not going back there!"

The Wookiee barked, for once in agreement with Lando.

"No argument," Leia said firmly, assuming the dignity of one accustomed to having her orders obeyed. "Just do it. That's a command!"

"What about those fighters?" Lando argued as he pointed to three TIE fighters closing in on them. He looked to Chewbacca for support.

But, growling menacingly, Chewbacca conveyed that he knew who was in command now.

"Okay, okay," Lando quietly acquiesced.

With all the grace and speed for which the *Millennium Falcon* was famed, the ship banked through the clouds and turned back toward the city. And, as the freighter continued on what could become a suicide run, the three pursuing TIE fighters matched its turn.

Luke Skywalker was unaware of the *Millennium Falcon*'s approach. Barely conscious, he somehow maintained his hold on the creaking and swaying weather vane. The device bent under the weight of his body, then completely broke off from its foundation, and sent Luke tumbling helplessly through the sky. And this time, he knew, there would be nothing for him to cling to as he fell.

"Look!" Lando exclaimed, indicating a figure plunging in the distance. "Someone's falling . . ."

Leia managed to remain calm; she knew that panic now would doom them all. "Get under him, Chewie," she told the pilot. "It's Luke."

Chewbacca immediately responded and carefully eased the *Millennium Falcon* on a descent trajectory.

"Lando," Leia called, turning to him, "open the top hatch."

As he rushed out of the cockpit, Lando thought it a strategy worthy of Solo himself.

Chewbacca and Leia could see Luke's plunging body more clearly, and the Wookiee guided the ship toward him. As Chewie retarded the ship's speed drastically, the plummeting form skimmed the windscreen and then landed with a *thud* against the outer hull.

Lando opened the upper hatch. In the distance

he glimpsed the three TIE fighters approaching the *Falcon*, their laser guns brightening the twilight sky with streaks of hot destruction. Lando stretched his body out of the hatch and reached to grasp the battered warrior and pull him inside the ship. Just then the *Falcon* lurched as a bolt exploded near it, and almost threw Luke's body overboard. But Lando caught his hand and held on tightly.

The *Millennium Falcon* veered away from Cloud City and soared through the thick billowing cloud cover. Swerving to avoid the blinding flak from the TIE fighters, Princess Leia and the Wookiee pilot struggled to keep their ship skyborne. But explosions burst all around the cockpit, the din competing with Chewbacca's howl as he frantically worked the controls.

Leia switched on the intercom. "Lando, is he all right?" she shouted over the noise in the cockpit. "Lando, do you hear me?"

From the rear of the cockpit, she heard a voice that wasn't Lando's. "He'll survive," Luke replied faintly.

Leia and Chewbacca turned to see Luke, battered and bloodied and wrapped in a blanket, being helped into the cockpit by Lando. The princess jumped up from her chair and hugged him ecstatically. Chewbacca, still trying to guide the ship out of the TIE fighters' range of fire, threw back his head and barked in jubilation.

Behind the *Millennium Falcon*, the planet of clouds was receding farther in the distance. But the TIE fighters kept up their close pursuit, firing their laser weapons and rocking the pirate craft with each on-target hit.

Working diligently in the *Falcon*'s hold, Artoo-

Detoo struggled against the constant lunging and tossing to reassemble his golden friend. Meticulously trying to undo the mistakes of the well-intentioned Wookiee, the little droid beeped as he performed the intricate task.

"Very good," the protocol droid praised. His head was on properly and his second arm was nearly completely reattached. "Good as new."

Artoo beeped apprehensively.

"No, Artoo, don't worry. I'm sure we'll make it this time."

But in the cockpit, Lando was not so optimistic. He saw the warning lights on the control panel begin to flash; suddenly alarms all over the ship went on. "The deflector shields are going," he reported to Leia and Chewbacca.

Leia looked over Lando's shoulder and noticed another blip, ominously large, that had appeared on the radarscope. "There's another ship," she said, "much bigger, trying to cut us off."

Luke quietly gazed out the cockpit window toward the starry void. Almost to himself, he said, "It's Vader."

Admiral Piett approached Vader, who stood on the bridge of this, the greatest of all Imperial Star Destroyers, and stared out the windows.

"They'll be in range of the tractor beam in moments," the admiral reported confidently.

"And their hyperdrive has been deactivated?" Vader asked.

"Right after they were captured, sir."

"Good," the giant black-robed figure said. "Prepare for the boarding and set your weapons for stun."

The *Millennium Falcon* so far had managed to evade its TIE fighter pursuers. But could it escape attack from the ominous Star Destroyer that pressed toward it, ever closer?

"We don't have any room for mistakes," Leia said tensely, watching the large blip on the monitors.

"If my men said they fixed this baby, they fixed it," Lando assured her. "We've got nothing to worry about."

"Sounds familiar," Leia mused to herself.

The ship was rocked again by the concussion of another laser explosion, but at that moment a green light began flashing on the control panel.

"The coordinates are set, Chewie," Leia said. "It's now or never."

The Wookiee barked in agreement. He was ready for the hyperdrive escape.

"Punch it!" Lando yelled.

Chewbacca shrugged as if to say it was worth a try. He pulled back on the light-speed throttle, suddenly altering the sound of the ion engines. All on board were praying in human and droid fashion that the system would work; they had no other hope of escape. But abruptly the sound choked and died and Chewbacca roared a howl of desperate frustration.

Again the hyperdrive system had failed them.

And still the *Millennium Falcon* lurched with the TIE fighters' fire.

From his Imperial Star Destroyer, Darth Vader watched in fascination as the TIE fighters relentlessly fired at the *Millennium Falcon*. Vader's ship was closing in on the fleeing *Falcon*—it would not be long before the Dark Lord had Skywalker completely in his power.

And Luke sensed it, too. Quietly he gazed out, knowing that Vader was near, that his victory over the weakened Jedi would soon be complete. His body was battered, was exhausted; his spirit was prepared to succumb to his fate. There was no reason to fight any more—there was nothing left to believe in.

"Ben," he whispered in utter despair, "why didn't you tell me?"

Lando tried to adjust some controls, and Chewbacca leaped from his chair to race to the hold. Leia took Chewbacca's seat and helped Lando as they flew the *Falcon* through the exploding flak.

As the Wookiee ran into the hold, he passed Artoo, who was still working on Threepio. The R2 unit began to beep in great consternation as he scanned the Wookiee frantically trying to fix the hyperdrive system.

"I said we're doomed!" the panicked Threepio told Artoo. "The light-speed engines are malfunctioning again."

Artoo beeped as he connected a leg.

"How could you know what's wrong?" the golden droid scoffed. "Ouch! Mind my foot! And stop chattering on so."

Lando's voice sounded in the hold through the intercom. "Chewie, check the secondary deviation controls."

Chewbacca dropped into the hold's pit. He fought to loosen a section of the paneling with an enormous wrench. But it failed to budge. Roaring in frustration, he gripped the tool like a club and bashed the panel with all his strength.

Suddenly the cockpit control panel sprayed Lando and the princess with a shower of sparks. They jumped back in their seats in surprise, but Luke didn't seem to notice anything happening around him. His head hung in discouragement and deep pain.

"I won't be able to resist him," he muttered softly.

Again Lando banked the *Millennium Falcon,* trying to shed the pursuers. But the distance between freighter and TIE fighters was narrowing by the moment.

In the *Millennium Falcon*'s hold, Artoo raced to a control panel, leaving an outraged Threepio to stand sputtering in place on his one attached leg. Artoo worked swiftly, relying only on mechanical instinct to reprogram the circuit board. Lights flashed brightly with each of Artoo's adjustments, when suddenly, from deep within the *Falcon*'s hyperspeed engines, a new and powerful hum resonated throughout the ship.

The freighter tilted suddenly, sending the whistling R2 droid rolling across the floor into the pit to land on the startled Chewbacca.

Lando, who had been standing near the control panel, tumbled back against the cockpit wall. But as he fell back, he saw the stars outside become blinding, infinite streaks of light.

"We did it!" Lando yelled triumphantly.

The *Millennium Falcon* had shot victoriously into hyperdrive.

Darth Vader stood silently. He gazed at the black void where, a moment before, the *Millennium Falcon* had been. His deep, black silence brought terror to the two men standing near him. Admiral

Piett and his captain waited, chills of fear coursing through their bodies, and wondered how soon they would feel the invisible, viselike talons around their throats.

But the Dark Lord did not move. He stood, silently contemplative, with his hands behind his back. Then he turned and slowly walked off the bridge, his ebon cloak billowing behind him.

☐ XIV

THE *Millennium Falcon* was at last safely docked on a huge Rebel cruiser. Gleaming in the distance was a glorious red glow that radiated from a large red star—a glow that shed its crimson light on the battered hull of the small freighter craft.

Luke Skywalker rested in the medical center of the Rebel Star Cruiser, where he was attended by the surgeon droid called Too-Onebee. The youth sat quietly, thoughtfully, while Too-Onebee gently began to look at his wounded hand.

Gazing up, Luke saw Leia, followed by See-Threepio and Artoo-Detoo, entering the medical center to check his progress and, perhaps, bring him a little cheer. But Luke knew that the best therapy he had received yet aboard this cruiser was in the radiant image before him.

Princess Leia was smiling. Her eyes were wide and sparkling with a wondrous glow. She looked just as she had that first time he saw her—a lifetime ago, it seemed—when Artoo-Detoo first projected her holographic image. And, in her floor-length, high-necked gown of purest white, she looked angelic.

Raising his hand, Luke offered it to the expert service of Too-Onebee. The surgeon droid examined the bionic hand that was skillfully fused to Luke's arm. Then the robot wrapped a soft metalized strip about the hand and attached a small electronic unit to the strip, tightening it slightly. Luke made a fist with his new hand and felt the healing pulsations imparted by Too-Onebee's apparatus. Then he let his hand and arm relax.

Leia and the two droids moved closer to Luke as a voice came over an intercom loudspeaker. It was Lando: "Luke . . ." the voice blared, "we're ready for takeoff."

Lando Calrissian sat in the *Millennium Falcon*'s pilot's chair. He had missed his old freighter, but now that he was once again its captain, he felt quite uncomfortable. In his copilot's chair, the great Wookiee Chewbacca noticed his new captain's discomfort while he began to throw the switches to ready the ship for takeoff.

Luke's voice came over Lando's comlink speaker: "I'll meet you on Tatooine."

Again Lando spoke into his comlink microphone, but this time he spoke to Leia: "Don't worry, Leia," he said with emotion, "we'll find Han."

And leaning over, Chewbacca barked his farewell into the microphone—a bark that may have transcended the limits of time and space to be heard by Han Solo, wherever the bounty hunter had taken him.

It was Luke who spoke the final farewell, though he refused to say good-bye. "Take care, my friends," he said with a new maturity in his voice. "May The Force Be With You."

Leia stood alone at the great circular window of the Rebel Star Cruiser, her slim white-draped form dwarfed by the vast canopy of stars and the drifting ships of the fleet. She watched the majestic scarlet star that burned in the infinite black sea.

Luke, with Threepio and Artoo tagging along, moved to stand next to her. He understood what she was feeling for he knew how terrible such a loss could be.

Standing together, the group faced the inviting heavens and saw the *Millennium Falcon* moving into view, then veering off in another direction to soar with great dignity through the Rebel fleet. Soon the *Millennium Falcon* had left the fleet in its wake.

They needed no words in this moment. Luke knew that Leia's mind and heart were with Han, no matter where he was or what his fate might be. As to his own destiny, he was now more uncertain about himself than he had ever been—even before this simple farm boy on a distant world first learned of the intangible something called the Force. He only knew he had to return to Yoda and finish his training before he set off to rescue Han.

Slowly he put his arm around Leia and together with Threepio and Artoo, they faced the heavens bravely, each of them gazing at the same crimson star.

STAR TREK

These are the voyages of the starship Enterprise...

Captain's log, stardate 1980.6:

Exciting adventures from television's most popular science fiction series, starring the legendary Captain Kirk, Mr. Spock, Dr. McCoy and the crew of the Enterprise—and of course, Klingons, Romulans, and Tribbles!

Exciting Space Adventure from DEL REY